Other Titles By

Angela Weaver

A LOVE TO REMEMBER

BLIND OBSESSION

BY DESIGN

BY INTENT

NO ORDINARY LOVE

TAKING CHANCES

Bound by
Knowledge

Bound by Moonlight

Angela Weaver

Parker Publishing, LLC

Noire Passion is an imprint of Parker Publishing, LLC.

Copyright © 2007 by Angela Weaver

Published by Parker Publishing, LLC
12523 Limonite #440-438
Mira Loma, CA 91752
www.parker-publishing.com

ISBN 978-60043-005-3

First Edition

Manufactured in the United States of America

Dedication

For my wonderful editing duo,
Angelique Justin and Deatri King-Bey...
Thank you for the inspiration and determination.
If it weren't for y'all kicking me in the pants and reminding me about my
deadlines, this book would still be in my head and not on the shelves.
Thanks also to Tarb for being a friend, an inspiration,
and a sounding board.

And always, my mom.
You are the best, even when I'm the worst.
I love you more than chocolate.

Prologue

Blake Holland sat underneath an old oak tree that stood next to the remnants of his mother's vegetable garden as he remembered the way she'd spent hours bent over with a hoe, tilling the soil and planting seeds. He shook his head slightly, remembering how his mother convinced him that gardening was a privilege and not a chore.

Drawing a deep breath, Blake's gaze swept over the place that used to be his home. The house looked dilapidated but had a nice front porch, and a stream going through the side yard that was concreted to channel the mountain run-off in the spring. His uncle had constructed a little curved bridge over the stream with a place for picnics hollowed out of the hill with stone benches and floor.

He remembered his Uncle James saying, "It's a big world out there, Blake. Got good people and plenty of bad. You gonna find it one day." Drawing in a deep breath of the cool air, he let it out of his lungs and watched the steam curl. For the past decade, he'd traveled the globe on business, sacrificing everything for this career. Since he'd left home for college, Blake had attained his master's degree in international finance, Jurist Doctorate, and become a member of the District of Columbia Bar. He'd parlayed all that hard work into the executive-level position as the Global Head of Trade at Citigroup Inc. But after successfully running the division for five years, he was leaving it all behind to start anew.

Blake tipped his head to the side slightly when he caught the sound of car tires crunching over gravel. Within a few moments, the car door opened and slammed shut, and he breathed deeply knowing that the faint sent of vanilla would hang in the air. A sharp wind cut through the air, and he was grateful for the hat on his head as he looked to see a smartly dressed young woman in an ankle-length wool coat walking in his direction. He watched her walk, and it was like looking in a mirror.

Bound by Moonlight

She possessed the same long legged self-assured stride, stubborn chin, light brown eyes and deep caramel skin.

Physically, they could have been identical twins, but mentally they were different on many levels. Not that any of that mattered. They had both discovered at a young age that only family mattered and only money could make things happen and garner respect. Although he'd only been six years old at the time, Blake could recall the hour of Caroline's birth because he'd been the one holding his mother's hand before and after the midwife's arrival. The screams and smell of blood had kept him awake nights, standing at the foot of his mother's bed, watching them sleep. He couldn't help but grit his teeth when he thought about how his sister's birth had been a shock to their small community. People couldn't get over the fact that Nadie Holland had birthed another bastard child.

He drew in a deep breath and focused on his sister's approach. "Morning," he called out.

"It's cold out here, Blake," Carolina said, coming to a stop a few feet from him.

"Just the way I like it."

"Why do you always come here?"

"Why do you insist on following me when you've got a husband to take care of?"

She shrugged and slowly moved to sit down. Blake narrowed his eyes at the way she carefully took a seat next to him under the tree. "Scoot over please."

Smiling at the childlike undertone of her voice, he moved to the right and let his little sister sit in the warm spot he'd created.

"Yesterday my team closed a fifty million dollar project with the Department of Defense. Tomorrow Scott and I are closing on a seven-bedroom, six-bath colonial brick in Prince George, and I'm up for another Image award this year. But why is it I still don't feel like I've got enough, Blake?"

"You don't yet. Give it seven months."

Her eyes narrowed. "Damn. I told him not to tell anyone, but that ass went behind my back. Wait until he gets back from New York tonight. He's going to be sleeping in the guest room."

"He didn't tell me anything, little sister. It's the end of winter, and your skin is glowing."

"Oh."

"Your husband isn't doing his job very well is he?"

"What does Mike have to do with this?"

"He promised me he'd keep you in check."

"I couldn't let you leave without seeing you, and I knew you'd be here."

"And how is that?"

"You always come back here when you're about to do something big. It's like you want Momma to see it."

"Maybe." He shrugged. "Or maybe I want to see how far I've come."

"Mike and I still can't believe you're actually leaving Citigroup."

He shrugged and looked away. A part of him had been reluctant to give up the salary and prestige he'd fought so hard to gain. But even as he drove his BMW through the newly revitalized town and turned right at the old church, his chest swelled with righteousness. Despite all the townspeople's predictions that the Holland boy would come to a bad end, he'd proved them wrong. Moreover, although she hadn't lived to see it, his mother would have been proud. "I've earned more money than I can spend in a lifetime, and it's gotten old. I needed a new challenge, and this is an opportunity to work on another level."

"And gain even more power and influence," Caroline added.

"There's nothing wrong with it." He grinned. As the head of the United States Trade Team, his mission was to settle a dispute over American construction industry exports to Japan.

"I just want you to be happy, and I would love it if you were close to home." She placed a gloved hand over her stomach and said in a low voice, "I'm terrified, Blake."

He softened and curled his left arm over her shoulder and placed his right hand atop her own. His mother had had a difficult time giving birth, and it had taken her months to recover. Blake wasn't a very religious man, how could he believe in a God that would punish the innocent? Yet, he still prayed to God for his mother and sister while asking the devil to damn his father. "I'll always be here if you need me."

"That will be a little difficult with the fifteen hour flight," she wirily replied.

Blake sat back and grinned. Both he and his sister were no strangers to international travel, but while marriage and pregnancy had restricted her business travel, his new position as chief negotiator for the United States Trade Representative office would lead to an increase in his time spent outside of the U.S. borders.

"When will you return?"

"Depends on the negotiations, a minimum of three weeks if the talks go well. Very rarely does the conference continue over the scheduled timeframe. But I should be there as little as three weeks or for more than a month."

"Do me a favor?"

"Anything," he said. There was nothing he wouldn't do for his little sister, and he knew in his heart she felt the same. Growing up, she'd helped him fight when they were teased at school because of their clothes or their being borne out of wedlock. Caroline had not only been his little sister, but his savior. There had been many nights that the only reason that kept Blake from running away from home was the thought of leaving her alone unprotected. He loved his little sister to distraction.

"Stay safe and try to have a little fun please."

"Where's the fun in playing it safe?" he teased.

Caroline sighed heavily with all the drama she could muster. "I'll miss you."

"Back at you." He pulled his little sister into his arms and kissed her on the top of her head. He recalled doing the same things numerous times when they were children. Kissing her goodnight, kissing the scraped skin, and wiping away the tears. He remembered playing in the stream, running in the woods and all the fun they'd had together. But he also remembered the cold walks to school, and the terror of her getting sick because his mother didn't have enough money to pay a doctor. Blake made a mental note to get all the names of the premier obstetricians and pediatricians and forward them to his sister's husband. Nothing would ever harm his sister. She was the only family he had left.

Vatican City, Italy

"I need you to go to Tokyo."

"What?" Dakota replied. She held her cell phone closer to her ear and put her finger in her other ear in a futile effort to block out the roar of the crowd. St. Peter's Square in the center of Vatican City was filled with a sea of humanity. Only minutes ago as the pope's death was announced, people fell to their knees and wept and sang. Standing alongside hundreds of her journalist colleagues, she'd been witness to the passing of Pope John Paul II. She'd been in the middle of an interview, when the news of the Pope's imminent death had been released. Not a person to be idle, she'd immediately gotten on the phone and picked up a contract to cover the unfolding story.

"Catch a flight to Tokyo," her bureau chief shouted. "You've been reassigned to cover the upcoming U.S.-Japan trade talks."

"You've got to be kidding me," Dakota snorted. "I'm in the middle of one of the most important events Rome has seen since Caesar's death, and you want me to watch paint dry at a trade meeting?"

"Trust me. It's going to be a helluva lot more interesting than paper shuffling. This is big, Dakota."

She shook her head. After having worked as a freelance journalist for the past five years, she'd learned the rules of her trade the hard way. It shocked her now that the man who'd taken her under his wing when she'd graduated would ask her to do something without first giving her details. "First rule of journalism: Never trust someone who says 'Trust me.' You should know that, Bert, because you told me that my first day."

Bound by Moonlight

With only a quarter of her attention on the phone conversation, her eyes continued to scan the area, taking in the range of emotions, the intensity of the moment. Although she'd adopted the more expedient use of a digital tape recorder, her hand still itched for a pencil and paper to write. She wanted to take in every small detail and paint the scene in words that would convey the enormity of the event.

She pressed a button, and began speaking into the machine while gesturing toward the photographer.

"It is an emotional day here in Rome. Young, old, believers and non-believers gather in St. Peter's square to mourn the passing of an icon," she said, and then gestured for the photographer to turn his camera lens toward the sight of a businessman cradling a grandmother as she cried. She had never been a very religious woman. Both of her parents believed in God. Her mother chose to worship in the way of her Sioux ancestors. Her father, raised in the South and brought up in the Baptist church, took Dakota to church on Sunday mornings. Yet although she believed in the presence of a Divine figure, the gruesome stories she'd covered during a two-year stretch of high-risk assignments had tarnished her faith in a benevolent God. Maybe that was why she remained impartial while the entire crowd grieved over the Roman Catholic leader's passing .

"Find someone else," Dakota barked, intentionally allowing her increasing annoyance to creep out. Her transition into investigative journalism didn't keep her from wanting to go back to covering assignments. But the nightmares and psychological stress of confronting horror, whether in investigative files, on war-torn streets or the bombed ruins of an apartment building, or in African streets red with blood kept her from going back. Once Rome finished mourning, she would return to the Finance Ministry and continue her questions. It would take her months before getting the information she'd need to link the ex-CEO of one of Italy's now defunct Banco di Roma to an American investment corporation.

"I can't. It has to be you."

"Why me?"

"I can't go into it over the phone. I've set you up to meet a contact in Tokyo, and he'll brief you on the rest."

"No. You've got to give me a better reason than it's big story. I trust you with my career, but this is going too far."

Bert's weary sigh stretched over the Atlantic. Dakota checked her watch and calculated the time difference. It was a little after five o'clock in the morning in New York City and knowing her boss, he'd probably just woken up from the pull out couch in his office.

"Fine. I didn't want to tell you this, but the assignment involves Peter Connor."

The conversation went from occupying part of her brain to a hundred percent with the mere mention of the man's name.

"What does Peter have to do with trade talks, Bert?"

"I'm not allowed to say anymore, but if you care about him, you'll be on the next plane to Japan."

Before she could question him any further, there was a click, and Dakota was left with the steady drone of the phone line. She swallowed past the lump in her throat and whispered, "Peter, what have you done?"

"Everything okay, Dakota?"

She turned and hastily constructed a smile as the photographer lowered his camera and walked to her side.

"I'm sorry, Jack. That was the bureau. I've been re-assigned, and I need to leave tomorrow. Can you stay for another hour and send the pictures back to news desk?"

"Sure. Anything specific you want me to try and take?"

"Try a few shots of the crowds from different angles. If you can squeeze in a few of the arriving officials, that would be nice."

"Will do."

Dakota gathered her belongings and made her way through the crowd of journalists toward the closest subway entrance. Vatican City had curtailed most vehicular traffic, leaving Dakota without the option of catching a cab. As her feet moved swiftly over the pavement, her thoughts shifted back to Peter Connor, the man she'd loved all her life. When he'd first come into her life, Peter had been fresh out of military

7

academy. As her father's protégé, he'd spent weeks at their house in the summers. Over the course of a decade, he'd left the armed forces and managed to become one of the most influential politicians in America. Poised to become the next speaker of the Senate and a possible vice presidential candidate in the next election, he couldn't afford the hint of scandal. Dakota stopped and stood to the side of the entrance to the subway as people poured up the stairs. No matter how many awards, honors, or titles Peter possessed, she'd only thought of him as her friend.

She looked up at clear spring sky and took it as a sign that she could be able to get a flight out. She blinked her eyes as memories flooded her, and she tried to keep the emotions at bay. Nothing would stop her from helping him; no matter what.

Chapter 1

Tokyo, Japan

It was ten minutes to midnight and the night's entertainment had just begun. As the band finished taking their places on the stage, Blake picked up his glass and relaxed in his seat. Within moments the first strum of the bass guitar echoed through the jazz club and an appreciative audience began to clap.

"Man, doesn't this place make you think you're back in the Memphis sitting in a local joint off Beale Street?"

Blake took a sip, and the alcohol relaxed him enough to grin at the comment. He chuckled. "Not unless your eyes were closed."

The irony of his comment wasn't lost on his colleague. Blue Note was nestled amid the skyscrapers and nightclubs in Tokyo's Aoyama District. Tonight's exclusive performance had come at the price of half a grand per ticket, but Blake would have paid more to hear Chantal Elliott sing. Dimmed lights and table candles cast shadows against the acoustically sound walls, and mirrors. He took a breath and the mingled scent of cigarette smoke and roasted meat. The jazz club was a complete replica of its sister club in New York, but the similarities ended with the clientele. Blake's eyes settled on row after row of suit-wearing Japanese businessmen. Efficiently maneuvering between tables were servers dressed in black, each holding a tray laden with alcohol and appetizers.

"Way to ruin a fantasy," Greg responded. "I haven't been home in over seven months. The other day I had a dream I was sitting in the backyard about to chow down on some ribs and potato salad. Man, I shed a tear when the alarm clock went off."

"You can go back anytime."

"Yeah, you tell that to the ambassador. He's riding everybody at the consulate hard. If I wasn't being assigned to your team, I'd be back at the office."

"You're welcome." Blake grinned and let his attention return to the stage. He had a few weeks before the trade conference began, and in that space of time not only would he prepare for his new role, he'd fulfill a promise and make an attempt to enjoy his stay in Japan. The headline singer took her place at the grand piano and began to sing. The woman's husky voice reverberated through his skin.

Greg dropped his glass on the table and sat forward. "I'm thinking that I'm starting to hallucinate."

"What?"

"Just walked into the room. Black coat."

Blake turned and followed the direction of Greg's stare. The woman entering the room caught his attention and his breath. Even from the distance, Blake thought she was the most beautiful woman he'd ever seen. Her tall, supple and perfectly proportioned figure demanded male appreciation. Yet all thoughts ceased when his gaze moved to her face and slowly connected with a haunting pair of eyes. The breath stilled in his lungs and everything faded. The music faded from his ears and the audience disappeared from his vision.

Her eyes were almond shaped, almost oriental and a gorgeous shade of brown. From his perspective, they were so dark he could lose himself in them and be perfectly happy.

His gut tightened and every muscle in his body seemed to tighten. Never before in his life had he been so profoundly affected by a woman. Her eyes darted away, and along with her male companion, she crossed the room to a small booth in the corner. Even when she'd left his field of vision, Blake continued to stare. The woman had been taller than a large percentage of the jazz clubs occupants; her black hair was pulled back into a ponytail that trailed over her shoulders, revealing dainty ears, an oval face with high cheekbones and full sensual lips. She wore a long coat so he couldn't see if she were wearing business clothes, or something more revealing.

10

Blake's hand tightened around the glass he held, trying to keep stemmed the tide of jealousy that poured though his veins as he recalled the woman had not been alone. He closed his eyes and focused on remembering her hands. Mentally picturing her long fingers, he breathed at the lack of a wedding ring. Whoever the man was accompanying his siren he was not\ her husband. Only a fool would let a woman like that walk around unclaimed.

"Do you know her, Greg?" he asked after a moment.

"No, but I know that guy. He's a manager at the Associated Reporter."

Blake frowned and swirled the rum in his glass. As much as the woman intrigued him, her connection to the media turned him off. As far as the public was concerned, Blake Holland was a self-made, educated, wealthy businessman turned government official. It was a familiar and well-liked story he wanted to maintain. Although the Defense Security Agency had conducted an extensive background investigation in order for him to gain the security clearance necessary for him to perform in his current position, no one outside of his sister knew the intimate details of his life before leaving Virginia.

He searched through his memories for any news correspondent or journalist who remotely resembled the beautiful woman and came up empty. The music changed, slowing down even further and deepening the mood. Something about the stranger drew him; piqued his interest and left a vision of her face running through his head. He took a drink of the aged rum. The smoky flavor filled his mouth and momentarily drowned his senses. Like it or not, he would make it his mission to find out more about the lady with the confident sexy stride and beautiful ebony eyes.

Dakota smiled at her friend as he held out her seat before sliding into the one at her side. They had an excellent view of the circular stage. "Thank you."

Because she'd spent years learning how to read people, she'd only needed the barest glance at Scott's face to see the attention-gathering entrance had upset him.

He ignored her stare and instead signaled to a nearby server. "I would like two scotches, neat."

The server frowned at the last term and Scott clarified. "No water, no ice."

The Japanese man nodded once and disappeared. Dakota sat forward and spoke in a hushed tone. "Scott, I don't drink Scotch."

"Yeah," her friend sat back in his chair, "I know. They're for me."

Her brow rose at the uncharacteristically curt response. "What's the occasion?"

"My impending termination."

"What?" Dakota sat forward in her seat. Inviting Scott to the concert had been an expedient way for her to get connected into the diplomatic goings on in Tokyo. She needed as much information as she could possibly gather. With the trade conference only weeks away, the clock was ticking.

He rubbed his brow and sighed aloud. "For Christ's sake, Dakota, you just practically stared down the chief negotiator of the trade talks."

"Is there something wrong with that?"

"It is when I'm trying to keep a low profile. If word gets out back at the office that I was seen with you, there's a good chance I'll be shipped to Moscow." He grimaced. "You know I can't stomach cold weather."

"What's the harm in a little friendly outing between friends?"

After the server delivered the drinks, Dakota ordered a sparkling water and tried to make small talk. Scott, however, wasn't having it. "Come on, Dakota. These tickets had to be what twenty or thirty thousand yen. A drink at a small sake house would suffice, but you've got to want something pretty bad to drop hundreds of dollars for such an exclusive concert."

She sat back and sighed. Scott was right. The tickets were expensive, and she did have an ulterior motive. But she wasn't coming out of her pocket for this. Every dime she spent would be charged back to her bureau, and she could care less where the accountants chose to allocate the items she placed on her expense report.

Unconsciously, Dakota frowned. It went against the grain that she would be here investigating one of the few people she trusted. Someone she'd grown up with. The man she would consider a brother if she hadn't been crazy in love with him for over a decade. Nothing would stop her from clearing the shroud of suspicions from Peter's name.

"Scott, I need to know if you've come across anything with Senator Peter O'Connor's name on it."

"Of course, he's in the news everyday."

"I'm not talking about anything public. I need to know if there's anything buried, anything whispered, rumors, accusations. Have you seen any hits on his profile? Anything besides his coming here to speak at the conference opening."

"Sorry, Dakota, I can't tell you. Even if I could, why would you want to discuss this here of all places with the key trade representative sitting less than a hundred yards away from us?"

"I have my reasons for being here."

"I'm sure you do, but I can't take that chance."

"We both know you could care less about being seen here with me. The Associated Reporter has you tied up with one of the most secure contracts every written. If you were an academic, you'd be tenured. So what or who is it that's keeping you from answering my question?"

"I can't tell you, Dakota"

She bit back a curse of annoyance. If this had been any other assignment, she could have sat back and pulled on the cloak of impartiality that came standard with her career as a journalist. But this particular story touched a very personal nerve.

Dakota leaned in over the table and tapped a bluntly manicured fingernail. "That's the second time in the last half hour you've said that exact phrase, Scott. Can you think of something a little more creative? How about I don't know? Or I'll tell you over my dead body. . Better yet, how about if I told you I'd have to kill you?"

"Don't you think I'd tell you if I could?"

"No, I don't." She shook her head. For one thing, she hadn't told him about the true reason behind her visit to Tokyo nor why it was important that she meet with Blake Holland. The second his name crossed her mind, Dakota's heart rate spiked. She'd chosen to meet with Scott at the jazz club that night because she'd known he would be there. "The person who pulls your strings is a lot higher up than anyone I know. So if you were given the order not to talk, you won't talk. But if I find out something you knew could have helped Peter, then there will be hell to pay."

"Look, I want to get away from this as fast as I can. If I can keep my nose clean for the next three years, I'm going to be running the San Francisco office. I've had enough of living in corporate housing and moving around every couple of years. I'm getting too old for this."

"Save it for your memoirs. I know you better."

"Look, ask me about the best places for sushi, the most crowded subway lines, the names of the Prime Minister's kids, but don't ask me about Peter."

"Fine. Tell me about Blake Holland."

"You don't give up do you?"

"I don't have a choice. I'm going to put down a card, Scott, and I'm going to trust that it will stay between us. Whatever is going to happen here involves those two, and since I can't get to Peter, I'm going to start with Blake."

"He'd clam up if he finds out you're a reporter. He doesn't take interviews."

"You're right, but I don't want an interview, I just want answers. And if I play my cards right, he might be open to giving them."

Halfway through the concert, Dakota turned to the left and glanced in Blake's direction. After waiting until she was certain that he'd caught her glance, she took a sip from the ice cold Perrier with a slice of lime. The false bravado that had propelled her to hold eye contact with Blake Holland had long since vanished. She'd seen his short camera interviews, looked at his photos, studied his bio with the thoroughness of a forensic accountant, but nothing could have prepared her for the stomach-dropping effect of his stare. She'd been blessed with what her mother called a third eye, and that special ability had come to the forefront the minute she'd stepped into the concert hall. Even before making eye contact with Blake Holland, she'd felt the weight of Blake's stare with every step they'd taken toward the table.

Even seated he had an aura of confidence, and her thoughts had become jumbled as she looked into those discerning brown sugar eyes that seemed to burn into hers and tear through her secrets. The shirt and tie he wore with a casual elegance could have been tailored to fit in all the right places. The symmetry of his bald head coupled with his strong brow and defined cheekbones...*Umph*, she inhaled deeply. A disquieting coldness about the planes of his defined face—the arrogant curve of his brow, took away from his handsome looks.

Dakota wrenched her thoughts from Blake Holland and stared ahead at the stage. As the songstress transitioned into another song, Dakota tapped her finger along with the beat. Tonight she would enjoy the music, and two days from now Blake Holland would finally meet his match.

Chapter 2

At a quarter past eleven at night, Blake finished the last page of the trade brief. He sat back in the chair and rubbed his eyes. Part of him wanted to go to bed; the other part still contended this was not time to sleep. He shook his head as all the small nuances of his new position came to mind.

He stood and crossed the expanse of the hotel suite to stare out the window. Tokyo's famous skyline papered with skyscrapers, office buildings and car-laden streets. The megalithic Tokyo municipal buildings clustered to his left. On his second day in the country, he'd been invited to take a tour of the city by car. It had taken the whole day, and by the time he'd retuned to his hotel, Blake had gained a new appreciation for home. No matter how much the city of Tokyo could be deemed a man-made wonder, the hills and mountains of West Virginia would never be eclipsed in his mind.

He looked over at the well-stocked bar and contemplated mixing a drink to help him fall asleep. But long ago he'd chosen to never drink alone. His thoughts turned down other avenues and stopped on the image of his mystery woman. Correction, he knew her name.

He looked over at the paper-laden desk and knew exactly where the copy of her reservation information sat. Even her name added to the mysterious attraction he found himself caught up in. *Dakota Montgomery.* Her name glided across his thoughts like silk. She'd arrived yesterday, and would be staying for two weeks. His unexpected actions of deliberately following her cab and being surprised that she'd pulled into the same hotel shocked him. He'd thought about following her up to her room and introducing himself, but instead he'd politely pressured the night manager to pull up her records and to keep him informed of her departure and arrivals from the building.

His conscience didn't even twinge at using his influence as the chief U.S. trade negotiator to get what he wanted. And what he wanted was an opportunity to meet her alone. The chance to see if the woman who'd caught his attention was as intelligent as she was beautiful. After being in the Washington scene for a few years, it hadn't taken Blake long to learn that beauty caught his eye but intellect kept his attention.

The phone rang, and he moved away from the window to answer it. Mentally, Blake calculated the time zone difference and tried to rationalize who would call him after hours, knowing that he was across the Pacific.

"We apologize for disturbing your rest, Mr. Holland. I am under instructions to call you should the guest in room 415 leave the room."

Blake glanced at his watch for a second time, and his brow furrowed. Although Tokyo was a large metropolitan city, it was not a twenty-four hour city like New York. "Did she leave the building?" he asked.

"No, sir. According to the computer, Ms. Montgomery is currently using the hotel's fitness room."

"Thank you." Blake returned the phone to the cradle and headed toward the walk-in closet. All thoughts of sleeping or reading more negotiation briefs disappeared. Within moments he'd exchanged his slacks, shirt and tie for more comfortable workout attire and gym shoes. He grabbed his key card and headed out the door.

During the ride down in the elevator, Blake attempted to rationalize his actions. It had been too long since he'd last enjoyed the presence of a beautiful woman, and Dakota Montgomery was a convenient excuse to satiate his physical needs. At least that was the reason Blake gave himself for entering into the large well-equipped exercise room.

Blake shook his head. Technically, he'd been up for two days. The sun had set hours ago, and it would be a few more hours before he got any sleep. Yet the sight of the lone woman sitting with her eyes closed awoke every nerve in his body.

He walked over to the weight bench and adjusted it for the chest press, then sat down. He grabbed hold of the weights, gritted his teeth and pushed. The muscles in his arms clenched and released. With a grin on his lips, he turned toward the still unmoving Dakota. "I've seen many people drift of into sleep during my meetings or in the middle of a golf tournament, but this is the first time I've seen someone fall asleep while lifting weights." His voice brimmed with amusement.

Dakota's eyes popped open, and she blinked at the sound of the masculine voice. The fitness room, which occupied half of the hotel floor, all of a sudden seemed small. She released her grip on the handles and watched Blake Holland stand and walk over to another bench. He settled into the leg press machine adjacent to hers. He adjusted the weights, pushed back the seat, and began to work out. His every movement smooth and controlled. The short-sleeved shirt revealed far more than all the images she'd seen of him.

Blake, she surmised, wasn't a stranger to hard work or a hard workout. Underneath the golden light of the room, Dakota could assess the man more clearly. His photographs had hinted to his physical fitness. But Blake's muscles showed in all the right places. Even at a distance, she could tell his abs would be firm to touch. The man in the flesh was much lighter than his publicity shots. His skin was a rich shade of burnished amber and just as flawless as the semi-precious stone.

All of him commanded her attention, but his eyes captured her thoughts. And the woman who manipulated words as a living didn't know how to respond to his impromptu greeting. Several heartbeats passed before Dakota shook her head with a small smile. "I wish I could really go to sleep that easily. But I can't tonight. And judging by the fact that you're here in the fitness room instead of your hotel bed, I believe you're having the same problems sleeping as well."

"Jet lag?" Pausing in the middle of the exercise, his legs almost fully extended, he studied her, apparently in no hurry to return the heavy plates to their resting position. His right eyebrow inched upward.

"With a vengeance," she enthusiastically replied.

She gave Blake a warm, open smile for the first time. The expression transformed her face, mesmerizing him with her natural beauty. Her hair was a rich, thick, raven black. It was pulled back and constrained in a ponytail that fell down past her shoulders. Her large eyes, framed by long slender lashes, were the same dark shade as her hair. He could only describe her complexion as smooth—an unblemished yellow-brown that reminded him of his native Virginia soil.

He laughed, and Dakota had to hold herself still as the sound echoed in the room. The right bass of it warmed her in a disarmingly familiar way. Only two men in the world had that affect on her: her father and Peter. She cleared her thoughts and stood up from the workout bench. She bit the inside of her cheek at the unexpected pleasure of the moment, but the reality of the situation reasserted itself in her mind.

Maybe if they'd met under different circumstances, the sparks flying between them could have sparked something more. Not that she needed to have more. She just wanted what she wanted, and in terms of the men in her life, no matter how wonderful they were, none had surpassed Peter in her eyes.

Blake left the machine, and within a few strides stood next to Dakota. His arm came up, and his hand was outstretched. "Blake Holland."

"Dakota Montgomery," she replied softly. She studied him for a moment before taking his extended hand, and the contact told her even more about Blake than his biography. He didn't have the soft hands of a businessman or an academic; he had a man's hands. The remnants of a few well-placed calluses that showed he didn't just supervise and reach into his wallet. Sometime in his past, Blake Holland had used his muscles more than his mind.

"Dakota," he repeated. "That's an unusual name."

"Especially for a woman," she added wirily.

"I take it you get that comment often."

"At least two or three times a week. There are days when I wish I could go by a middle name."

"Good option. But something tells me you choose not to take it."

"No," she shrugged lightly. "I don't have a middle name."

His eyes widened in surprise, and Dakota had to look away as her heartbeat lost its steady rhythm. At that moment, small warning bells sounded somewhere in the darkness of her psyche. If she couldn't even look Blake in the eyes, how would she work alongside him in the upcoming weeks?

"Did you enjoy the concert last night?" he asked.

She nodded. "Very much so. And you?"

"You couldn't tell by my enthusiastic standing ovation?"

"I noticed." She smiled. "I'm just surprised you remember me being there."

"A beautiful woman such as yourself would be hard to miss, especially in Tokyo. I was in the back with a friend."

She nodded. "There aren't too many people of African descent here, are there?"

"Just a few. But it's very welcoming to see."

"So where are you from, Blake?" Dakota asked as she switched machines. Asking a question to which she already knew the answer gave her a needed conversational distraction from his earlier compliment.

"Born and raised in a small town in West Virginia. What about you?"

She aimed a well-placed sideways stare in his direction. He had to be kidding. "Can't guess from the name?"

Blake nodded, his grin instantly drawing her eyes to his mouth. "I'm not a gambling man. And if I did, I would need to have better than fifty-fifty odds."

Intrigued by the frank admission, Dakota reached up and brushed back a stray strand of hair that had worked itself out of her ponytail. The more they talked, the more she realized that all the documents, newspaper clippings, interviews, comments from personal references and professional colleagues couldn't tell her what she really needed to know about him.

"I grew up in North Dakota."

"Guess the time change difference had you pretty hard."

"Less than I expected. I took a direct flight from Rome. Everyone was flying into the city and not out. The plane was empty, and I took advantage to lie down and sleep. Now I'm dealing with the consequences. My body clock has turned upside down and inside out."

"Flew in from Rome, huh. Are you here for business or pleasure?"

Dakota stood up and made her way to the opposite side of the room toward one of five treadmills. With every step, the hairs on the back of her neck tingled with the knowledge that Blake's eyes were on her. When she reached a machine, she turned and leaned against it. "Business."

"And how long will you be staying in Tokyo?"

She met his glance, and her stomach dropped. The hint of masculine interest she thought she heard in his voice was confirmed by the warmth of his dark eyes. Dakota had quickly come to discover that without trying and without even subtly making moves at her—which men did frequently—Blake Holland had her mesmerized. Even after being in the same room for a half an hour, she didn't want to know about his relationship with Peter or the trade talks, she only wanted to know about *him*. She only wanted to study the little nuances of his face and listen to his voice.

"I'm not sure. I guess as long as it takes for me to complete my assignment."

"And what's that?"

She fixed him with a bright smile and winked. "It's confidential." She stepped onto the treadmill.

Blake finished his last repetition and stood up. Dakota dropped her eyes to the console and pressed the start button, fully aware of his presence when he claimed the treadmill on her left side. With a feigned light tone, Dakota turned to Blake and asked, "Are you here on business as well?"

"Yes. I'm here for the upcoming trade talks."

"Ah, the final push to avoid going before the World Trade Council." As soon as she said the words, Dakota instantly wanted to pull them back. No matter what happened that night, tomorrow morning when she met with Blake's boss, the budding possibilities would end, but she wished she could have held on to the moment longer.

"You're either very well informed or you're involved."

Dakota cleared her throat and avoided looking in his direction. "Maybe it's a little bit of both."

Bound by Moonlight

Seconds later, a hand reached across her treadmill and pressed the stop button. The belt slowed to a stop. She barely had time to get her balance before she stood face to face with Blake. He was so close that all she had to do was stand up on her tiptoes and their lips would touch. Part of her mind worked furiously to find a way to diffuse the explosive tension, while the other half, the part of her that enjoyed rushing into unknown and potentially dangerous situations wanted to add fuel to the fire by kissing and nipping the strong curve of his chin. She inhaled his masculine scent, stared at the slight pulse of the vein under his neck. His hand wrapped around her forearm like a vise.

"What are you doing?" she asked coolly.

"Who are you, really?" he demanded, his eyes appearing a darker shade of brown as they narrowed on her face.

When she didn't answer immediately, he grabbed her other arm and gave her a quick shake. "Better yet, how long have you been spying on me?"

"Release me, Blake," she said in a hushed tone. Her heart furiously beat in the back of her throat.

"You already knew who I was, didn't you?"

Dakota had learned how to play poker long before she'd gone to elementary school and spent break time playing go fish. Her father and his friends had allowed her into the sanctuary of their Sunday card games. And so as she stared up into his eyes, she could have confidently lied. "Yes."

"I'm going to ask one last time before I make a phone call and make your stay in Tokyo very uncomfortable. Who are you and what are you doing here?"

"I'm a journalist with the *American Review*," she said proudly even as his fingers tightened. "Now, let me go."

He dropped her arm as if she were diseased and took two steps back. Although she hid it well, the look of contempt on Blake's face hurt worse than she'd ever admit. Knowing he disliked the press, she'd been prepared for anger and annoyance, but not the look of disappointment that flickered across his expression. Someone, somewhere had burned him, and every sin would be heaped upon her shoulders.

She opened her lips to say more, but his look stopped her cold. Between one breath and the next, he strode away. Dakota leaned against the treadmill and drew a shaky breath. Blake Holland wouldn't make it easy. She straightened and got back on the treadmill. Too bad, she sighed heavily. She was a sucker for doing things the hard way.

Chapter 3

N ext time, at least give me a last meal before feeding me to the sharks," Blake announced.

Ben Michaels regarded Blake Holland on the conference room video monitor before replying. "Against policy to feed the animals."

Settling back into his seat, he barely acknowledged the small television camera that sent his image halfway around the world via satellite video-conference technology. Ben knew he took one of the biggest gambles of his career last year on Blake Holland. Strategic thinking and godlike patience were the prerequisites in their realm; an impartial nature and pragmatic, and, a little too confrontational and too blunt Holland would never be a model diplomat. He'd learned Blake wasn't a big team player.

At Citigroup, where he'd been hired right out of graduate school into a senior business level position, he'd managed to earn a reputation of making major changes overnight in a company lambasted for its inability to adjust to new technologies. Yet, when a global banking scandal threatened to topple the bank and destabilize the international monetary system, it was Blake who managed to get all the necessary countries to the table. When the conference ended five hours later, Citibank's stock soared, and the foreign exchange markets stabilized. The president of both the World Bank and the United Nations counted Blake Holland as a friend.

The Secretary of State hadn't batted an eye when Ben had placed Blake's file on the table as a replacement for the former trade negotiator. If there were a way to successfully pull off the Japan trade conference and uncover Peter O'Connor's involvement, it was Blake. The man's integrity was unquestionable, business acumen unmatched, loyalty and resilience unwavering. He had an uncanny ability that was pure genius, developed at the World Bank, where he learned how to maneuver as a pawn as well as a player. Blake had a knack of manipulating the odds to his favor, and that's exactly what he needed the most right now.

"I'm not going to mince words. Whatever you've got against journalists, get over it."

Ben Michaels, Blake thought, proved that one should never judge a book by its cover. He looked like an NFL football player in a Brooks Brother's suit. In reality, he was brilliant, charismatic and manipulative as hell; jock was the last adjective that could ever be used to describe him. He came from a family of international financiers, diplomats and statesmen. He was a legend around the world, having brokered some of the most complex trade agreements in history. It had come to no surprise when the newly elected domestically focused president had wanted someone else to take the lead in crafting foreign and economic policy, Ben was chosen as his chief advisor. If anyone could handle a potential trade war or political confrontation that could harm the current administration, it was Ben. The question in the equation was how the beautiful woman he met last night fit into the equation, and how could he get her out of it?

Last night as Blake lay in the bed with an erection that wouldn't go away, he'd remembered little things about Dakota...like her hair sweeping gently over her brow as she leaned forward, listening to his tutoring. When he'd turned over to stare at the alarm clock all he could think about was the way her eyes, the color of rich chocolate, framed by long black lashes and delicately arched brows, widened when she smiled.

He'd been attracted to her before he'd even spoken to her. But seeing her up close had kicked up his libido to a high level of lust. All he'd wanted to do was kiss her and see if her mouth would taste as welcoming as it looked. He'd watched her work out and with every movement, a primal hunger had welled up deep inside him and his hands had itched to run his fingertips over her bare flesh. His tongue wanted to taste her skin while the rest of his body wanted to have her long legs wrapped around his back as he sheathed himself in her wetness.

He knew he wanted the lady in the worst way.

He also knew he was flat out of his mind.

A smart man would forget about the moment they'd stood inches apart and he'd watched her eyes darken with attraction. An intelligent man would erase the memory of how close he'd come to kissing her. But he hadn't kissed her last night.

The realization should have brought him some relief.

It didn't.

Now he would have to work with her. Be with her for hours at a time. Unclenching his teeth, Blake asked, "Why Dakota Montgomery?"

"Why not? She's good at what she does."

"She's an investigative journalist, not a correspondent. If you want someone to report on the conference without getting a whiff of the scandal, she's not that person."

"This is one of the reasons why we need her. She's smart and relentless in her pursuit to uncover the truth. Her father barely made it out of Vietnam alive, and she, just out of undergrad, went back to unearth one of the biggest military cover-ups of the decade. After she got her master's degree, she went off to Africa as a war correspondent. She's spent time in Beirut, Lebanon, Gaza and Afghanistan. I've been told she got burned out and came back to the States." Michaels rapped his pen against the desk. "Since then, she's been approached by the Secret Service and the C.I.A. for operative positions, and she's turned them down cold. Personally, I don't think they could control her anyway."

Blake barely managed to keep his expression blank during Michaels' speech. Although they were communicating via satellite video feed, the increase in technology was almost as if they were face to face. If he concentrated he could see the shadows of an early sunset in the background. In actuality, he'd learned very little about Dakota during their brief conversation in the fitness room the night before and what had been most important hadn't been verbal. Michaels rarely gave praise, but the chief counsel to Trade Affairs hadn't even bothered to hide the fact he was more than impressed with Dakota Montgomery. "What has all this got to do with the trade conference?"

"Always impatient. I'm getting there. As I said, Dakota has connections to a few high level members of the senate. We need her access to one person in particular. Senator Peter O'Conner."

Blake frowned as he instantly recalled the young senator from Illinois. If the rumors were correct, he was on the short-list to be the next vice-presidential candidate. The senator was set to give the closing speech at the trade conference.

"If I didn't know you better, I would think you were hedging," Blake said.

"They halfway grew up together. Colonel Montgomery, Dakota's father, and Peter's father went off to war, her father came home from Vietnam and his didn't. Peter's mother died shortly afterward, and he was enrolled in boarding school. He spent most of his summers at the Montgomery ranch. Being that Dakota's mother died when Dakota was in high school, the two bonded closely. According to the analysts, Dakota is the only person except for her father who Peter trusts."

Blake crossed his arms over his chest and narrowed his eyes at the conference screen. "I've met Peter O'Conner, Michaels. He's a politician, a potential vice president and the opening speaker for this conference. That's all; he doesn't have the access to confidential information, so he can't be the leak. If there's some favor you need to ask, task to be accomplished, then ask me and I'll do it. I don't need a journalist snooping around when I've got intensive negotiations coming up."

"Evidently I haven't made myself clear enough, Holland. You're going to work with Dakota because we need you to. An undercover defense operative managed to identify the senior analyst responsible for passing information to the Japanese. We've managed to isolate the analyst and reassign him to a less sensitive area without causing suspicion. And that led to the situation we're in now. If Peter O'Conner isn't handled properly, your negotiations with the Japanese will fail, and not only will the construction go in their favor, but this will strain an already fragile economic alliance. Through some highly classified conversations, the C.I.A. has passed on the information that the main source behind this is Nobu Toshinori, head of a Japanese construction firm with ties to the *Yakuza*, a Japanese organized crime syndicate. One of his trusted American lackeys was seen talking to Senator O'Connor this morning. Time is running out, Blake. We need Dakota to get close to Peter, find out what Toshinori has over the senator and neutralize the situation. I've contacted the head of the Bureau of Diplomatic Security, and the local agents have been briefed on a need to know basis. My only stipulation is that a team of D.S. special agents be with you at all times. Good luck."

Blake nodded grimly and left the room.

"Peter O'Conner is on the verge of committing treason."

Dakota stared at the man on the video-conference screen as if he'd suddenly grown another head. After an unscheduled 7:00 A.M. wake-up call, room service, chauffeured drive to the American Embassy and a damn near strip search to get into the building, this was the final straw.

"You're insane, Mr. Michaels. What possible reason would Peter have to participate in espionage? He's rich, politically connected and a possible candidate for vice-presidency. I've known the man half of my life."

"And you're in love with the man, Ms. Montgomery."

Every word stopped in her throat and heat crept up Dakota's neck and into her face. "Excuse me?"

"This wasn't a last minute decision on our part to choose you for this assignment. There had to be extraordinary measures taken within my organization to reach out to a civilian and a journalist at that. We've interviewed many of your colleagues, past acquaintances and had a team of experts examining every aspect of your life. And it all boils down to the evidence supporting your affection for Peter O'Conner, and it seems that you and your father are the only two people he would ever trust."

"Did you propose this to my father?"

"No."

"Because you know he would never betray Peter."

"That is correct."

"But you expect me to?"

"I expect you to get to the truth regardless of whether or not it implicates Senator O'Conner

She shook her head. "Someone is trying to set Peter up, and I won't stand here and let that happen. This conversation is over." She started toward the door, pulled it back and encountered two suit clad men on the other side.

Director Michaels' voice called out from behind her. "I'm sure you don't want to leave yet, Ms. Montgomery. We haven't finished our discussion."

Dakota didn't move a muscle. "I think I've heard more than enough."

"Traveling abroad as a U.S. citizen is a privilege, not a guarantee. Your career requires the ability to travel all over the world. What would happen if by chance your passport was revoked or if your name happened to show up on Homeland Security's No-Fly list?"

Her teeth clenched at his threat. She could have taken three steps and pushed past embassy security, but at a high cost. Although Dakota had promised her father she would avoid taking assignments in war zones or hot spots, she never planned on taking a desk job in New York. "You bastard."

"Sit down," he ordered calmly. "Hear me out, and if we can come to an agreement, you'll be allowed to leave."

Dakota's eyes turned from fire to ice. "You mean if I do what you want, I may be able to keep my job. Don't spin this, Michaels. You're not the only one with psychological information. I've read about your career, and I'm fully aware of what you're really capable of doing."

"Good, so then you know what lengths I'll go to serve the interest of my country."

"You mean the interests of your political backers."

"In this situation, they both happen to be the same. Now will you sit down and listen to me?"

Dakota aimed one furious stare at one of the guards as he gently closed the door in her face. She didn't have a choice. Even if she could manage to keep Michaels from canceling her passport, his influence around the world could hinder her effectiveness as a reporter.

"Six months ago, we intercepted a few messages from the Japanese ministry of international trade that negotiations might go badly if there wasn't some sort of outside intervention. We stepped up monitoring and engaged the assistance of Echelon."

Although her expression remained neutral, Dakota's mind raced at the confirmation of the existence of the intelligence-gathering program. Rumors about Echelon had floated around journalist circles for decades. She'd heard that the supercomputers were programmed with a "dictionary" of key words and could combed millions of intercepts picked up by listening posts around the world. If everything about Echelon was true, then a defense analyst in Washington could eavesdrop on a cell phone conversation in Moscow within a matter of minutes.

"Three months ago, it seemed that all communications regarding the trade conference ceased, but we did manage to pinpoint one person who seemed to be in a position of power to be able to access and distribute that kind of information—Peter O'Conner. All the intelligence was passed over to the State Department and the senator has been under constant surveillance since then."

"And what did you find?"

"That he's been meeting with Nobu Toshinori. A millionaire Japanese businessman with a taste for expensive toys and who has known ties with the Yakuza."

"The man is rich, probably a contributor to Peter's campaign funds. That's not enough for you to think he's going to sell out his country."

"Even you know that argument doesn't hold water, Dakota. Take off the glasses and get your head in this situation. Whether you like it or not, Peter's interests at this meeting are suspect. If he's going to pass along information to the Japanese that could weaken our power, then we need to know now and neutralize that threat."

"I take it this is where I come in?"

"Yes, you are going to be the bait."

"What?"

"By placing you in a position with direct access to the chief negotiator. Peter will come to you for the information he needs."

Dakota rubbed her brow and wished she'd been able to sleep last night. All the jogging and weight lifting hadn't been enough to keep her mind from churning, her thoughts from returning to Blake Holland.

In her dreams last night, she'd lain naked. Some how the cotton sheets had transformed to Blake's hands slowly and gently touching her body. His fingertips gently, so gentle they barely touched her skin, ran the course of her back, along her side and dipped into the crevice between her thighs. All the while she'd watched him slowly work his way back up to her breasts. He'd circled the erect orbs with the palms of his hands and fingertips. He'd kissed around her breasts, driving her crazy with the desire for him to touch her nipples. A shiver racked her body, and Dakota reached up to wipe the back of her brow with her hand. Although the conference room climate control was set to a degree above freezing, the sheen of perspiration lay on her skin. Fighting to push away the memory, Dakota asked Michaels, "Why would he come to me?"

"He'll have no other choice. We've been carefully screening out anyone within the trade administration Senator O'Conner may have had any contact with and left nothing to chance with the information pertaining to the conference. Everything is on a need to know basis. Only myself, Blake and a few senior members have knowledge of our trade strategy."

Dakota drew back in her chair as all the pieces of the puzzle came together and punched her in the gut. From the very moment her editor had ordered her to Tokyo, she'd assumed Blake Holland was somehow the threat to Peter. Now, everything had changed and she in essence could be sending the man she'd fancied herself in love with years ago to prison. "And so he'll come to me?"

"Officially at the behest of the U.S. Trade Representative's office, you are writing an unprecedented exclusive in-depth documentary on the conference. Unofficially, it's been circulated that the administration is

31

using this even to elevate Blake's stature in the administration, by assisting in writing his story."

Dakota flashed back to the look Blake had given her the night before. *Dislike.*

She'd felt it in the marrow of her bones. She shook her head. "This is not going to work, Michaels. Obviously, you don't know Blake Holland that well. He has a definite aversion to people in my industry."

"That may be the case, but when it comes down to business and in this situation because it's a matter of national interest, Blake will accomplish his task."

Almost as if speaking the man's name had summoned her nemesis, the doors to the conference room opened, and he strode inside the room. Her lips tingled from the memory of how close they'd come to kissing last night. Dakota gripped the arms of the leather chair and remained focused in an attempt to hide how much the sight of him affected her.

He took the seat on the opposite side of the table and stared straight at her.

Damn it, he wasn't going to make her feel uncomfortable. She forced herself to make eye contact and with a little more nudging managed an artificial smile. "Mr. Holland."

His smile was equally false and didn't get close to his eyes. "Ms. Montgomery. Pleased to see you again."

"If you're going to be a real diplomat instead of a businessman, Mr. Holland, I highly recommend you learn to lie better."

"Sheath your claws, Dakota," Michaels ordered.

Dakota returned her attention to the screen. "Why?"

Her daring tone pulled a smile from the man across the table.

"Blake doesn't want to do this anymore than you."

Dakota's gaze fixed upon Blake's cold eyes. "You're not adverse to journalists are you?"

"I have never had an aversion."

"Because if you are," she leaned over and placed her palms flat on the table. "I can always go home."

He sat forward and placed his hands on the table, close, but not touching hers. "No need. What about you? Will you let your personal relationship with Senator O'Connor cloud your judgment?"

Awareness flickered in her eyes, but her tone was still even when she answered. "I'm a professional. I can do whatever the assignment calls for."

"Good. That makes two of us."

Their words hung in the air between them, took on a second meaning. Currents of sexual tension thrummed in the space between their eyes. Dakota moved her hands away, but Blake caught them. The gleam of unmasked hunger in his eyes sent a shiver ripping through her chest.

"Good." He stood up and came over to her side of the table. Dakota stood as well. She couldn't help but notice he was taller than her by more than half a foot. Used to being eyelevel with most men, his height coupled with the fact she was well aware of him physically put her at a severe disadvantage. "What's in your suitcase?"

"Excuse me?" Her brow furrowed.

"In order for you to make this cover story solid, I need you with me at all times until the end of the trade talks. In order for you to fit, you'll need an appropriate wardrobe."

"I'm a journalist, not an escort. Find someone else to provide arm decoration, Holland." Dakota shook her head. "I came to work not play."

His fingertips reached out, and not so gently forced her chin upward. She narrowed her eyes and met his steely stare with a defiant look of her own.

The deep bass of his voice reverberated across her skin. "If you want to keep your friend out of Guantanamo Bay, you'll do what I ask. My assistant has set up appointment at the appropriate salons. We leave for the clothing boutique in an hour. In the meantime, I recommend you read through the brief Michaels prepared for us."

"*We?*" she repeated incredulously. Her coal-black brows pulled together. The more time she spent in this place, the more ludicrous the situation seemed to become. "I don't need a babysitter. I've been here before. I'm perfectly capable of dressing myself."

"From now on either myself or a consulate escort will be with you at all times," Blake deliberately emphasized the tail end of the sentence. He wanted to throw her off balance just the way she'd turned his thoughts upside down.

She jerked her chin from his grasp and stepped away. "You think I'll warn Peter."

"I think you'll do whatever it takes to keep him out of trouble, but that's not all. You're also a potential target now that you're working close to the team. You've also been moved to a hotel suite adjourning mine."

Her furious glare only heightened his feeling of satisfaction. She didn't like this arrangement anymore than he did. He was relaxing now, despite earlier misgivings that made him want, at least partially, to turn around, pick up the phone, call Michaels and tell him to call off the mission.

"You're enjoying this aren't you?" she bit out.

Against his will, the corners of his Blake's mouth rose. He tilted his head and inhaled unconsciously, savoring the delicious, scent of desire beginning to stir warmly from her.

"I don't need a chaperone."

"Make sure we're clear." Blake took a step forward and looked down into her upturned face. "I won't let anything or anyone jeopardize this conference."

Twenty minutes after leaving the conference room, Blake responded to the tenth email of the morning. Although his mind should have been on finishing up the final details of his opening speech, he was staring at the closed confidential folder—Dakota Montgomery.

Know thy enemy, Blake mused. However, he hesitated at the thought of viewing the beautiful lady as an adversary. An irritant or a thorn in his side, yes, but he couldn't call her an enemy when they shared a common goal and played for the same team.

He put his hands behind his head and leaned back in the leather chair. To be honest, he was at loose ends and his mind balked at the thought. In his former life in the financial industry, he was used to cutting deals, spearheading change and actively making moves. Since becoming the U.S. trade representative, he'd spent the majority of his time relearning everything he knew about economic and trade policy, regulatory agencies, strategy and leadership.

Leadership, Blake thought, *more like clean up duty*. The powers that be didn't want to upset the apple cart by accusing a U.S. senator of spying; yet, at the same time if they didn't find a way to control the situation, a newly recovering American economy could slip back into recession. As much as he tried to concentrate on the latest economic outlook report, his mind kept wandering down the hall to Dakota Montgomery.

Closing the report, Blake leaned back in his leather chair, picking up his pen. Normally, flipping it between his fingers would clear his thoughts. But it had no effect on the image of her raven hair, beautiful eyes and stunning body.

The physical attraction wasn't unexpected. She met all of the criteria and added in a few things he didn't even think of. But there was more to the attraction than his need to possess her body. It was her fierce intelligence, the challenging spirit and sense of humor that kept him from being able to focus on his work.

"Uh-oh. The man has gone Japanese already, and you haven't even been here a week. I hope that the latest round of trade delegate requests isn't the reason for the look on your face."

Blake placed the pen on the desk and motioned Greg into his office. "This might come as a shock, but the conference is the last thing on my mind right now."

"Good," Greg responded emphatically, taking a seat in one of the black leather chairs in front of the cherry-wood desk. "Half a dozen trade analysts, three foreign service loaners, four translators and a few private consultants focused entirely on this conference should ease your mind.

35

Bound by Moonlight

So, now that I think about it, there could only be one thing that's got the legendary cool and confident Blake Holland spinning pencils."

Blake raised an eyebrow and smothered a grin at the cat-that-ate-the-canary look appeared on Greg's face. One of the very first things he noticed upon transitioning from business to government was the dire importance placed on information. When billions of dollars and man-hours were spent on the quest for information, the price of knowledge became exorbitantly expensive and created a clear line between the haves and the have-nots. From the smug look on Greg's face, his friend felt like he was in possession of a million-dollar tidbit of information related to Blake.

Blake stiffened as he imagined what it was. Abruptly, he left his chair, walked across the office, and shut the door. "Talk to me."

"The scuttlebutt rife is there's a brown skinned perfect ten sitting in the conference room. I took a peek from the video control room, and I swear she looks like the woman from the jazz club the other night."

"She is. Her name is Dakota Montgomery."

"What's her security clearance, and is she single?"

Blake walked back behind his desk and sat down. "She's a civilian and unavailable."

"That's harsh."

He narrowed his eyes and sat forward to emphasize his statement. "It's a fact. Ms. Montgomery is a journalist from the World Press. The Trade Department has asked her to write an in-depth article on the trade talks with a focus on the team."

"You have got to be joking?" Greg's mouth fell open.. "They let a journalist in the building without sending out a notice? What the hell is Washington thinking? It's like sending a fox into the hen house. By the time the conference is over, every diplomatic protocol, confidential trade document and top secret cable will be on the front page of the *New York Times*."

Blake shrugged and sat back. Of all the things he could possibly worry about, Dakota revealing classified information wasn't one of them. His only reservations revolved around her relationship with Senator

O'Connor. If she had a weak spot, that would be it. He could tell in that one brief meeting the man meant a lot to her. Unconsciously, his teeth clenched, and Blake fought down a wave of jealousy.

"I didn't make this decision. I'm just following orders. If it makes you feel better, we've placed her under twenty-four hour surveillance, and she will have an escort when she's in the embassy."

"Great," he replied. "That will help me sleep better at night."

"It should. Ms. Montgomery is my responsibility."

Greg shook his head as he stood up. "Good luck. You're a better man than I could hope to be. I won't even try to lie about my intentions. For a chance to spend some time between those lovely arms, I'd spill my guts and my momma's secrets."

Blake threw his head back and laughed out loud at the thought of what secrets Greg's mother could possibly keep. "I'll keep that in mind. And, my friend, this conversation is between us."

"Yeah, I got it—on pain of death and chewing cyanide and that stuff. Makes me feel like I'm some kind of C.I.A. agent instead of a diplomatic paper pusher."

"Thanks," Blake said, picking up the phone to call his assistant. It looked as if his schedule would have an unexpected opening.

Blake glanced at the clock. Her two hours were almost up. He really didn't have to accompany Dakota on her shopping trip. He could assign on of the staffers or authorize a diplomatic service escort.

Her file at a F.B.I. office, labeled Confidential had been handed to him as he walked though the embassy doors that morning. He spent only a few moments looking at her pictures. A few minutes before Greg's visit, he'd managed to scan through a few pages about her. All the facts and clipping from her newspaper articles were like pieces of a puzzle, and as with each new piece of information, the hazy picture of the fearless journalist became more apparent. She had a condo in Washington, D.C. she rented out to a friend.

An only child of an Army colonial, she'd gotten high scores on all of her IQ tests. He knew from her file that she flew home three times a year: her father's birthday, the anniversary of her mother's death from cancer and then Christmas. However, much information he gleaned from the list of Dakota's accomplishments and personal meetings. It was the men, or lack there of, that intrigued Blake.

Was it because of Senator O'Connor? A beautiful and intelligent woman like Dakota did not have to ask any man twice for company. Blake sat back in his chair and stared at the door. Knowing she was only a few yards away didn't ease his desire to see her nor calm his irritation at the role she played in the operation.

He looked at the file, opened it and paused on the first photo. Her picture hadn't done her justice. He paged through the other folders. The flat two-dimensional likeness taken by a combination of sources hadn't captured the energy that sparked around her, the incredible allure. He tapped the Monte Blanc pen against the desk and wondered if he should read more.

If her investigative report were similar to the others he'd read in the past, the remaining contents of the folder would contain everything thing there was to know about Dakota Montgomery. He would discover her family, where she traveled, notes on what she wrote, who she met. If he read her file he would learn what she ate, what she wore, how she voted in every election. Those details would tell him about her, but what he really wanted was to see what Dakota Montgomery was all about.

Decision made, Blake pushed back the chair and put the file in his briefcase.

Chapter 4

Washington, D.C.

Senator Peter O'Conner pushed his hands in the pockets of his trench coat and drew in a deep breath. When he exhaled, the fog of his breath disappeared in the February morning breeze. With the combination of a wide-brimmed hat and sunglasses, even his long-term Senate staff members would not have recognized him. Standing outside of the American History Museum, he stared into the horizon as his conscience tried to come to grips with why he wasn't in his office preparing a speech for tonight's part fundraiser.

"Early as usual, Senator. Such a rare and wonderful thing to have in any elected official."

The familiar nasal tone made Peter curl his fingers in his pocket. Nobu's overpaid handler had arrived. Peter barely glanced to the approaching man. Instead of responding, he began to walk toward the line of trees and benches. Although confident he wouldn't be recognized, with re-election and a possible vice presidential nomination in the near future, he couldn't afford to take chances.

Annoyance tightened his jaw at the predicament he'd found himself in. Although he'd been left with a substantial trust fund after his parents' death, that money alone could never have financed his senate campaign. Nobu Toshinori's financial backing and political maneuvering had helped him not only win his Congressional seat but gained him the ear of influential senior senators and department heads.

"Just think. In only a few short weeks, the cherry blossom trees will bloom, and this place will be packed with tourists. Wasn't that a wonderful gift from our Japanese friends?"

Peter gave the man a sideways glance, then shrugged off his sunglasses. "Cut the small talk. What do you want?"

Bound by Moonlight

"Our inside person to the U.S. Japan trade conference negotiations was re-assigned at the last minute. Mr. Toshinori has requested you provide him with a copy of the strategy. Once we have the document, or if you could provide a summary, Mr. Toshinori will make sure the sordid details of your time as an officer in Japan never see the light of day."

Peter almost tripped at Howard's request. He came to a dead stop and turned to look the man in the eyes. "Hell no. I won't give into blackmail, and I won't sell out my country. I'm just going to go forward with my past relationship and hope my constituents understand."

Howard nodded, and the cruel smile sent a shiver of foreboding over Peter's spine. "Don't you think the people I work for considered that?"

Howard pulled an envelope from the inside pocket of his sport coat and handed it to Peter. "Open it," he ordered.

Peter pulled it from his hand and ripped it open. His brows furrowed at the picture of a woman and a boy. As he studied their faces, the blood drained from his face. The little boy had his father's eyes.

"Congratulations, Senator O'Connor. You have a son. If you want him to live long enough to meet, you'll do exactly what I want."

Peter's mouth opened and closed as his heart raced. "Son of a bitch."

"Someone will contact you with the meeting locations after your arrival in Tokyo." Howard grinned, then walked away.

How? Peter's mind raced and his knees trembled. With shaky hands, he reached into his pocket and withdrew a small pill case. The acid rolling in this gut caught fire. He swallowed two tablets and sat on the closest bench. Toshinori had him by the balls, and he knew it. His career couldn't take the scandal, and he could never ignore the existence of his son. Peter closed his eyes, and his father's face shown like an after image against his eyelids. The thought of his father cut to the heart of his conflict. The most prized artifact in his million-dollar Georgetown townhouse was the gold Medal of Honor his father received for his service in Vietnam. He opened his eyes and looked down at the picture.

I have a son.

The shrieking bus tires announcing the arrival of the first wave of tourists broke his thoughts, and he turned again to look at the rows of cherry blossom trees. As the sun crept higher in the horizon, Peter realized with a sudden grim fatality, the clock had started ticking. His trip to Japan would commence in less than seventy-two hours. Three days to keep from betraying his country or losing his career and the son he'd never known he had.

Chapter 5

C ome closer, Dakota." Blake spoke from the edge of the room where he sat, with his legs crossed, in a sleek, black leather chair.

Startled, she did the exact opposite of his request and stopped. Each time she'd tried on a dress and gave into the Japanese woman's urging her to walk into the room, Blake had just looked up from his seat nodded and went back to typing on his laptop.

This was the fifth dress she'd tried on, each garment as stunning as the next. This one seemed to be a culmination in style as well as beauty. Dakota had always looked good in black, but the cut of the material, the fix of the dress and the quality of the thread seemed to make the dress a must-have. The length stopped halfway down her thighs, showing off her long legs. She'd had her doubts when following the saleswoman into the back of the store and into a bedroom-sized dressing room, but it had only taken her a glance at the selection of dresses, pants and skirts that had been pre-selected for her reservations to vanish. Dakota traveled around the world and visited exclusive boutiques, but she'd never purchased, and since there were no price tags and they seemed to be the only clients, this place screamed money. She'd never be able to afford any of the items on her salary.

"Come closer," he repeated. His voice held an edge to it. Something dark and so compelling, she'd taken two steps further into the room before stopping.

"Turn."

He was looking at her with a direct stare, deeply penetrating, evaluating, and appreciative. The pulse in the back of her throat jumped. Dakota fought the urge to turn around and walk back into the dressing room. The black silk dress moved across her body like a second skin, and as much as it concealed, it also revealed. The sensation of the material's coolness, coupled with the heat of Blake's stare on her cold skin sent ripples up and down her spine.

She lowered her gaze, took a deep breath. "Time is ticking, Holland. Can I have a yes, no, or next?"

She heard a thump and, fed up with the silence, she turned to leave. But before she could move, Blake blocked her exit. "The answer to the question is all the above, Dakota."

"I don't understand."

"Yes, I will take the dress. No, you will not wear it tonight."

She blinked twice, yet couldn't draw her eyes from his hooded gaze. While alone in the conference room at the embassy, she'd thought about Blake. About what she wanted to say when she saw him next. She'd imagined the conversation and planned what she would say and how she would act. But all of her mental precautions melted.

Blake continued, "You'll wear the silver dress tonight. I'll have the others sent to the hotel. I also want to see two more dresses."

"Why should I not wear the dress?" She aimed a pointed glance toward the room's recessed floor to ceiling mirrors. "I look good in this dress." It wasn't just the sight of the dress and the way it clung to her curves that made her mouth go dry; it was the sight of them. It was the reflection of Blake's hungry stare, the feel of him standing within a foot of her. In the mirror it looked as though they were touching, overlapping and mesmerized.

"I did not say that you wouldn't wear the dress, Dakota," he replied huskily. "You *will* wear the dress."

He turned her around fully so she was facing him. In the high heels, she had but to slightly tilt her head back to look him straight in his eyes. The desire etched on his face sent a swift rush of desire to the intimate parts of her body.

While her mind struggled for an appropriate verbal response to his behavior, she was silent. He took her silence for acquiescence, for his hands moved from her arms to her waist, slowly stoking from the top of her side down to the curve of her behind and rested on her hip in a way that was both possessive and soothing. Dakota stared, blinking into their reflection, seeing her own dilated pupils in the mirror as he held her there tight. Inches from his body. Waiting. Never in her life had Dakota felt so out-of-control and breathless with anticipation.

She followed the progression of his mouth as he lowered his head.

"You will wear this dress only for me," Blake whispered, his mouth just above her neck, so hot, so close. His breath against her skin made everything shiver. She had time to draw a quick breath; then his mouth settled on hers, kissing her forcefully, almost punishing her mouth. His tongue pushed against her lips and forced its way into her mouth. A moan shivered up from deep within her belly and stopped in her throat.

Dakota's eyes fluttered wide, and then shut. He held her there with one hand, cupped her hip and pulled her into even more intimate contact while his other hand traveled with achingly tender slowness up her spine to the nape of her neck. His long fingers brushed over her shoulder before journeying down to the curve of her breasts, easily slipping under the dress.

He stepped in closer, keeping his mouth on hers as his thigh slid between hers, and he pressed close enough so she felt the solid evidence of his arousal against her hip. Heated fingertips moved teasingly over her lightly padded bra, while her nipples rose to his touch, sending a swell of desire throughout her body, and weakening her knees. Her closed hands opened and lay against his chest, her fingers clenching and unclenching against the lapels of his jacket as the softly lit room faded into a hazy oblivion. She reached up to hold onto his shoulder as her tongue darted in and out of his mouth.

Only the sound of her own harsh moan snapped Dakota back to reality.

How could a man who so blatantly disliked everything about her, do *this* to her? Blake had made no secret that he disliked her based on her profession. She'd never forget the moment in the gym when the smooth light-hearted banter abruptly ended, and his eyes grew cold. She had witnessed similar behavior at the embassy. Yet, here in a small showroom boutique in the heart of Tokyo, alone with Blake Montgomery, her tongue ran across his full lips, his mouth consumed hers, his fingers pinched her nipples, her body pressed itself against the evidence of his arousal and she couldn't deny the desire for his fingers to discover the pearlescent wetness pooling within the apex of her thighs.

Flooded with doubts about both his actions and body's reaction, Dakota pushed against the rocklike wall of his shoulders and broke free of his kiss, almost falling with the abruptness of her freedom.

Her fingers reached up to touch her swollen lip as she tried to slow her rapid breathing.

Her chin lifted in false bravado. "What just happened?" Her voice came shakily over the space she'd created between them.

"Exactly what should have happened in the fitness room the other night. What I wanted to have happen the night you walked into Blue Note." His eyes were dark and shadowed, giving away nothing of his thoughts as they rested on her face.

Dakota drew a shaky breath and ran her hands down the material as if to wipe away the memory of his hands. "Never touch me again without my permission, Holland."

"You liked my touching you, Dakota." The deliberate calculation in his eyes sent an erotic shudder through her body. Drawing in a deep breath, she nodded slowly. There was no reason, nor did she have the ability, to deny his statement when all she had to do was look down at her own fully erect nipples to view how much her body had responded to him. "That doesn't matter. I don't mix business with pleasure, especially when the person in question is someone I don't trust."

"Trust takes time," he commented off-handedly

"Yes." She nodded and studied him. Studied him as she'd never done before. She searched his face for a tattletale twitch or movement; she studied his body language for any kind of sign. Something, anything to help figure out how a man who had disliked everything about her could do with a complete 180-degree change in attitude.

"The problem is I don't have the luxury of waiting for us to build trust for you to break. I will make no bones about the fact I don't like your profession, but it's not the profession I want. I want the woman."

"Sorry, I'm not on the menu." Dakota shrugged her shoulders without the least bit of sincerity. She wouldn't let it show, but the fact that he expected the worst of her before they'd even exchanged the most minimal of details about each other stung. She'd felt the passion of his kiss and the heat of his hands to the very center of her being, but it was too intense and too soon. "I'm only here to make sure that Peter doesn't get blamed for something he didn't do, not to get involved with a power hungry egomaniac."

Ignoring her angry stare, Blake continued to hold Dakota's clenched hand and placed a kiss on her knuckle. She wanted to turn around and run from him, scream at him, she wanted to do something other than stand there as the erotic feel of his tongue on her skin made her stomach knot into a ball.

His hooded gaze never left her face. "A car will be waiting outside when you're finished getting ready."

Dakota took a small step back and focused on balancing in her high heels. As she stood, she was almost eye level with Blake, and that small change in position gave her the confidence she needed to ask, "Are you loosening my leash or testing me, Blake?" Earlier he'd said she would effectively be under guard, not he'd seemingly reversed his decision.

"Call it a first step toward building that trust."

"Am I allowed to call Peter?"

His jaw tightened. "Don't press your luck, Dakota."

"It ran out the moment I got the phone call from my editor," she retorted.

"Funny." He grinned, then turned away and walked toward the door. "I thought the same thing until today."

Unwilling to scream at his back, Dakota pivoted on her heel and stalked from the room. How had she known he was a man who liked to get the last word? Oh, well, what did it matter? She would get the last laugh.

Chapter 6

Dakota took the champagne flute from Garrick Landon's hands as she half-listened to his latest excursion into the Japanese countryside. Blake had said he would be attending the reception, but he hadn't put in an appearance even though it was after nine o'clock. As she examined her newly manicured fingertips, she couldn't help but be extra sensitive to his absence.

She shifted most of her weight on her left leg. She'd thought her little ordeal would be over after parading the dresses in front of Blake at the boutique. But instead of taking her back to the hotel after she'd changed into her own clothing, the car had taken her to a professional salon for a manicure and pedicure. After a short trip, she'd ended up right back at the embassy ensconced in a small guest room with a box of clothing, shoes, incidentals and make-up. After a quick shower, she'd changed into her evening attire.

Although she'd loved playing dress up as a child, the novelty of it had worn off quickly after spending time in Third-World countries. What was most jarring was the infinite gap between the rich and the poor. On one hand, some of her graduate school colleagues had come from money, the kind of inherited wealth that guaranteed income just for breathing. On the other hand, she'd spent days living in villages where the water came from a well, the roof was barely thatched and animals roamed inside and outside of the huts. The thought brought back the discomfort she'd always felt when attending events such as the one she was at now.

"I'm not that much a shoe man, Montgomery. But those high-heeled shoes you're wearing and that dress might give me some kind of fetish."

Dakota looked at Garrick as if he'd grown another head, and he burst out laughing.

"What?" she said after his words registered.

Bound by Moonlight

"I knew you weren't listening. What's happened to the eagle-eyed reporter I met years ago?"

"Her hearing started to go from being around too many exploding mortar shells."

"I heard you'd been in Afghanistan. No wonder you decided to get out of that circuit and work in more civilized climates."

Dakota eyed the milling groups of high-ranked diplomats and business leaders. There wasn't any doubt in her mind that many of them would stab their best friend to get ahead. One thing she appreciated about the time in the field was that friends and enemies were clearly defined, and the fighting was out in the open. As a member of a close-knit community of African-American journalists, it made her proud to know that they actively chose to help rather than hinder each other. And it was times like these when she was a minority within a minority that she felt the most isolated. She pointed her pinky finger to the left at the French ambassador. "Oh, yes I feel really safe. I've had three offers since I walked in tonight, Garrick. The first was for a midnight rendezvous, the second was a getaway to an industrialist's villa in Tuscany and the third was from a Korean diplomat who offered me an undisclosed sum to gather intelligence on Ambassador Stewart."

"Maybe you shouldn't have worn that dress."

The fitted waist of the black, silk, sleeveless dress clung to every curve of her slender frame. Its low-cut front and open back showed off her long slender neck and graceful shoulders, while the above knee length displayed her stocking-clad legs.

It hadn't taken her long to realize he'd chosen it for the purpose of being provocative. Although she could have covered the revealing neckline with a cashmere scarf, she'd decided against it. Her plan was to give Blake exactly what he wanted, but she would never allow him to touch. With her free hand, Dakota reached up and touched the ebony wood disc pendant that fell right above her bust line. As always, the mere touch of it soothed her with a memory of who had given it to her. She closed her eye for a moment and sighed. Peter had brought it back from a trip to India. Sometimes she wished she could go back to the days when

48

things between them were simpler. It would have been easy for her to blame all her failed relationships on the fact that she was still in love with Peter. But that would be a lie. She loved Peter, but that emotion was of a familial not passionate nature.

She arched a freshly shaped eyebrow. "Maybe you shouldn't have written that article on the Russian diplomats gambling debts. Is it true they've barred you from entering the country for the next ten years?"

"You heard about that?"

"Everybody knows."

"Damn. I think I need another drink. You?"

"Still sipping." She smiled.

Garrick walked away at the same time the back of her neck began to prickle. Under the guise of taking a sip of her champagne, she peered out over the rim and scanned the room. Her small smile froze as her gaze met Blake's across the room. The low lighting honed the planes of his face and seemed to reflect back into his eyes, giving him an almost dangerous look. So used to hiding her femininity in order to gain respect in her career, it felt like a new toy, and she wanted to play with it. The only problem was Blake's intense response. For the first time, she wondered if she hadn't gotten in way over her head and unleashed a response far beyond her wildest expectations. The idea was thrillingly satisfying as it was frightening.

Another dignitary approached Blake, and the breath she hadn't realized she'd been holding was released. She swallowed and inhaled deeply while willing her pulse to slow. Only then did she detect the head of a body standing close to hers and the sandalwood scent of man's cologne.

Turning slightly, she glanced over her shoulder and encountered the dark gaze of a handsome Asian gentleman. His custom-tailed gray charcoal suit and matching tie lent him a European air.

"The night is only beginning," he stated without preamble. "But I would be deeply disappointed if the most beautiful woman in the room left before I invited her to dance."

His gaze burned into hers and his cool, confidence piqued her interest. She tried to place his accent and failed. His upturned eyes bore into hers with an intensity that threatened to make her self-conscious. "Mr. ..."

"Toshinori," he supplied. "Nobu Toshinori." He held his hand out in greeting. His voice was as smooth and deep as a ranch hand soothing a skittish mare.

Tilting her chin, Dakota flashed a polite smile. "Dakota Montgomery. I'm flattered for the invitation, Toshinori-*san*."

"Please call me, Nobu," he requested with an attractive grin.

"Nobu." She started to give an excuse to keep from dancing with him, but her eyes locked on Blake's familiar back as he danced with another woman. Returning her gaze to him, her lips curled upward in a welcoming smile. "I would love to dance."

He took her glass and placed it on a passing server's tray, and then placed his hand on the small of her back and led her into the mix of couples on the dance floor. By either luck or design, he chose the section furthest from Blake.

It was only after she'd rested her hands on his shoulders and fell into the rhythm of the music that he spoke. "So Ms. Montgomery. Are in Japan for business or pleasure?"

"Please call me, Dakota. I'm here for business. And yourself?"

He laughed, and the deep sound made the hair on the back of her neck stand up.

Her brow creased. "Did I say something funny?"

"No." He shook his head. "It's just refreshingly rare to meet someone that doesn't assume that I'm from Japan."

"I try not to assume anything. Not to mention, you're accent isn't giving me any clues."

"I was born in Ibaraki prefecture just north of Tokyo. My father was a diplomat, and I traveled around a lot and went to school in California."

"Hence the lack of an accent," she surmised.

"Yes. Now I've returned to Japan to run the family business."

"And if you don't mind my asking, what business are you in?"

"I work primarily in the construction industry. And yourself?"

"I'm a journalist."

"Here to cover the trade talks I assume?"

"In a way. My assignment focuses more on the personal side of the conference rather than the diplomatic maneuvering." Dakota had learned early on in her career to tell the truth whenever possible. Lies were messy, and she'd seen way too many of them come back to haunt the person who'd told them.

"My family has been involved in construction since the rebuilding after World War II."

She glanced upward as a chill worked its way down her spine. Dakota had never been one to believe in coincidence. "Sounds like you have a stake in making sure things go well."

"We all do." His fingers tightened on her waist. "I'm sure you're hoping Senator O'Connor has a successful story to tell the American people. It would be a significant blow to his campaign if things were to go badly for the U.S. trade team."

Her eyes narrowed at the veiled comment. "The senator has a very strong platform and voting base. I agree that it would hurt him if things didn't go well, but I'm sure he'd recover."

Nobu's lips curved into a slightly mocking smile. "It is a universal rudeness to talk politics with a beautiful woman after hours. Would you forgive me if I did so now?"

"That depends on the content of our conversation," she replied with a smile.

"I have an offer to make to you, Dakota."

She made eye contact with Nobu and held it. If ever she'd had her doubts that the man was involved with the plot to get the trade documents, they were erased that instant. Nobu Toshinori might have the mannerisms and accents of an international businessman, but he had cold, mercenary eyes.

"I'm listening."

"My family's history has been well documented in Japan, yet my company, although it is well-known here, I would like to establish our name on a more global scale. In order to accomplish my goal, I'd like to ask for your help. You will be more than adequately compensated, of course. And you would only need to interview my uncle and a few key members of the staff."

"Nobu, I am flattered."

"Good."

"But..." Dakota couldn't finish her sentence as he swung her back for a dramatic dip at the end of the song.

She smiled and when he pulled her upward, Dakota noticed all eyes had turned to them. Her cheeks flushed.

"I would hate to take no for an answer."

"I would need to speak with the Representative Holland first. I am here on assignment," she pointed out.

"I'll send a car to your hotel in the morning, and we can further discuss this over breakfast. I'm sure the representative is a reasonable man and will allow you to eat."

Dakota nodded and smiled. "You're very determined, aren't you?"

"I get what I want, Dakota." He took a step back and bowed low.

"I look forward to seeing you tomorrow."

She watched him make his way through the room toward the exit. Pasting a smile on her face, she moved back into the crowd and took her time reconnecting with the people she knew. Even while chatting and networking, her mind kept repeating her conversation with Nobu. Yes, Nobu wanted something, but it sure as hell wasn't her journalistic expertise. Her instincts were screaming that the encounter was a set-up. Even the pretext of hiring her to write a story on his family didn't add up. The only logical explanation was he'd known who she was and had an idea about why she was in Tokyo. Another piece of the puzzle had just landed on her plate. She sighed and fought the urge to rub her neck.

When she returned from the bathroom a few moments later, her eyes fell on Blake. For a moment, her eyes followed him as he moved through the room. His manners were excellent, and he focused his full attention on the people around him. In the space of seconds, he managed to win their approval and pull their interest like moths to a flame.

Damn, she cursed internally as she found her eyes locked on Blake. She'd spent most of the evening trying hard to remain focused on the reason for her presence at the reception. But nothing seemed to keep her from thinking about him.

Blake... the heat of his lips as his tongue had plunged into the recesses of her mouth. The strength of his shoulders beneath her clasped hands...the thought of him made her knees a little weak and sent a delicious shiver through her body. Dakota's mouth went dry.

Don't do this to yourself, Dakota, she told herself. Mentally shaking herself, she pushed Blake and pushed the memory of their kiss into the corner of her mind. She reached up, smoothed a tendril of her hair back from her face and returned her attention to the Australian ambassador. The music started up again, and the couples began drifting back into the main salon. Pleading that she needed to rest for a moment longer, she excused herself and headed outside. Dakota needed to talk to Peter and now.

The lady was unbelievable.

In the midst of the dozens of women in the room, his eyes instantly zeroed in on her. Blake watched Dakota strolling around the large reception room, passing coolly from one man's arm to another. Even among the pomp and circumstance of the Tokyo consulate party, she stood apart in a way guaranteed to garner male appreciation and female envy.

It fit that Dakota seemed to be completely at ease in the diplomatic circle. Since she'd been in the journalism industry about the same amount of time he'd been in the business world, he imagined she'd spent a lot of time attending parties. No doubt she would have easily gotten herself on the invitation list, even without his help. Event planners and public relations sought out journalists, and it didn't hurt that she was beautiful, intelligent and unattached.

Bound by Moonlight

She looked beautiful in the reception room. With the room being illuminated by a half dozen crystal chandeliers, the soft light only enhanced the color of her dress. In a roomful of women wearing the latest Italian dresses, expensive jewelry, and salon-perfected hairstyles; Dakota's simple, yet revealing, dress made a fascinating contrast. Her dark hair pulled back in a French chignon, leaving only a wisp of a bang that teased him to tuck it behind her ear.

Hormones threatened to overwhelm the logical side of his brain. For an instant, he had a vision of her naked, on her knees with her hands clutching the sheets and head tossed back. He could feel the silken strands of her hair in his hands as he rode her to climax. She'd be fire in a man's arms. Making love to her would be hot and wild, no control and like taking a freefall into flames. Damned if he didn't get an erection, and the desire didn't decrease as he watched her work the room.

He took a drink of the expensive brandy and savored the fiery burn down his throat and heat flush in his stomach. Maybe if he drank enough, it would deaden the hard-on he'd had since kissing Dakota at the boutique. Releasing a sigh of frustration, Blake set his half-full glass on a tray, which was carried by a black-jacketed server, and declined a replacement. He needed to keep his wits about him for the evening.

The conference was more than a week away, the senator had yet to re-confirm his arrival time and the Japanese Ministry of International Trade had yet to show signs of a softening position. Yet with all the complications, nothing could bring him to return to his duties and circulate amongst the diplomatic set. Instead, his gaze remained on the lovely feminine specimen wearing the revealing dress he'd chosen.

He'd been watching Dakota since he'd arrived, and he'd made certain that she knew it. But far from the open and welcoming smile she graced foreign dignitaries, American investment bankers and other invitees, she'd made a point of not looking in his direction.

A moment later, his friend Greg stopped by his side. "Damn, Blake. I have seen a fair amount of world-class beauties in my life, but Dakota is making every last one of them look like Cinderella's evil stepsisters. Did you know she was in the running for a Pulitzer Prize?"

"No," he responded with a casualness he didn't feel. Her file sat on his desk, and he had yet to read it. But Greg's information hadn't come from an NSA database; it had come from Dakota's lips.

It bothered him, he realized. Dakota bothered him. But what bothered him more was that he didn't mind the increasing amount of time he'd spent actively thinking about her.

Greg continued. "She's straight up fine. Are you sure, she's not available? Technically, she's not a part of the embassy staff."

Blake finished his drink and placed it on a passing server's trey and lifted two champagne glasses, then turned to Greg. He clapped him on the shoulder and didn't smile. "Listen closely. This is a one time only message: Dakota Montgomery is off-limits."

Tired of waiting for her to come to him, he purposely crossed the floor and followed her outside to an adjacent waiting room.

"Maybe I shouldn't have chosen that dress for you to wear."

Abruptly snapping shut her mobile phone, Dakota slid it into her purse and straightened at the husky tenor of Blake's familiar voice. She hadn't heard the sliding door open. Her sleeveless dress was midnight black silk, knee-length and cut simply with a revealing neckline in the front and low back. "You wanted me to get attention," she said matter-of-factly as she turned her head.

"Mission accomplished," Blake replied dryly as their gazes clashed. "I heard about your arrival even before I made it through the door." He held his right hand and gave her a glass identical to the one in his hand.

She automatically took the crystal flute of champagne and barely managed to turn her eyes from him. He wore a black pinstriped suit jacket with a white shirt, silver cufflinks and black tie, which made him look all the more powerful. The jacket, cut so it fit close his broad shoulders and muscled body to perfection, and the trousers accented his muscular thighs and long legs. However, even the elegant clothing didn't hide the raw power of the man underneath.

"So were you speaking with O'Connor?"

He watched her reaction to his question with interest. The confident mask slipped a little, giving him a glimpse of...not fear. Wariness maybe. She took a sip of the champagne and Blake sucked in a breath. Watching her lips curve around the thin glass made his skin burn with the thought of her mouth on his skin. And then she tipped her face up, smiled at him boldly. "Wouldn't you just love for me to say yes?" Her voice dripped with mockery.

"I'd love for you to say yes to sleeping in my bed tonight. But I'd rather not see O'Connor's name on my daily report without my knowledge of the conversation. The objective is for O'Connor to come to you for information, and we want you to be close to him, but I need to be aware of *all* of those calls Dakota."

The smile melted from her lips, and he caught a flicker of something in her oval dark eyes, there and gone too quickly to be identified. "You're tracing my phone calls?"

"I will know about every person you come into contact with and every move you make if I'm not with you. I will know everything you do, Dakota, until the end of the conference."

"Why am I being treated as a criminal, or Peter for that matter? Not once in all the meetings and documents I read was there a solid shred of evidence to support this witch-hunt."

"Save the speech and answer the question. Were you talking to Peter just now?"

"Why don't you read about it in your report?"

"I'd rather you tell me."

Dakota let out a small growl. "Fine, I left Peter a voicemail telling him I was here in Tokyo. Are you satisfied?"

"Not even close," he replied. "But I'll have the transcript of the call tomorrow."

"Distrustful, aren't you?" She looked at him with a new appreciation. In his place she would have done the same.

"As you mentioned earlier, trust isn't something that is given; it must be earned."

She was about to turn away when she felt the latch on her watch let go. "*Merde,*" she cursed in French, struggling to hold onto both her purse and the watch.

"Don't move. I'll fix it." She heard his spoken command at the same time he came to a stop in front of her. They stood so close she could feel feel the heat of his breath against her skin. Two inches and she would step on his feet. Dakota let her arm go limp as he held her wrist in his grasp. Biting her lip, she tried her best to ignore the goose bumps running up and down her skin as his thumb caressed the pulse of her wrist.

He pulled her closer and pushed against her mouth until her lips opened, and he drank the taste of her. The sweetness of the champagne and her flavor electrified his senses. Passionate. Sensual. Her tongue mated with his and swept into his mouth. The act went straight to his erection—stronger than his favorite mistress and was twice as potent.

Her body melted against his.

Dragging his mouth from hers, he found himself distracted by the sight of her tongue darting out to lick her bottom lip, as if she wanted to drink in every drop of the kiss.

"I want you," he breathed the words in her ear, even as he filled his lungs with the scent of her sexy perfume. "But I don't want quick meals or an appetizer. Don't think you can sleep with me once and walk away. If we allow this to happen, it won't be a one-time affair, and things could get messy."

Throat suddenly dry, Dakota tipped her glass to her lips and forced herself to stand straight. She'd felt each word like a physical punch, but not for all the money in the world would she let him know just how much they made her want him even more. Yet, her anger was self-directed. She'd known what she was getting into when she'd first learned she'd be working with Blake.

Peter's friendly hugs or her ex-boyfriend's for the matter hadn't affected her that much. If she had understood then what she'd been stepping into before getting on the plane from Rome, she still would have done the same thing. Pulling her annoyance around her like a coat, she straightened her back and gifted him with a cold smile. "Think what you like, Holland. I'm not that attracted to you now, later or ever. What the hell makes you think I'd ever agree to sleep with you?"

He grasped her elbow and began guiding her toward the main salon. "Because your body betrays you, Dakota. And mouths may lie but kisses never do."

Chapter 7

After a silent ride back to the hotel, Blake walked into her suite while unbuttoning his shirt. Dakota had just bent down to remove the strap of her heels. Forgetting her aching feet, she stood frozen, his parting words echoing in her mind. Every time he touched her, her body went up in flames and took every self-protective instinct she possessed along with it.

"You cannot just walk into my room like that." A feeling of desperation rose that had nothing to do with their deal.

She was talking to his shirt covered back as he walked over to the mini-bar.

"At first, I didn't want this either. But after tonight, I've got a better appreciation of the benefits of having you close," he said, opening a full decanter of scotch.

"Your benefits not mine," Dakota pointed out.

"I would think you'd show a little appreciation for the upgrade."

Dakota blinked. This was the first time she'd returned to the hotel since leaving this morning. And truth be told, she hadn't paid any attention to the fact that her new accommodations were in an entirely different section of the hotel and on a higher floor. She'd thought her view from the other hotel room was nice, but this guest room had a breathtaking view of the Tokyo skyline.

She took in the hotel suite in one glance. Everything was modern and stylish. A flat screen TV hung against the wall, hardwood floors and Berber rugs, high ceilings and marble stone countertops along with exquisite artwork and accents.

Taking off her other shoe and tossing her purse on a side table, she walked toward him and nearly bumped into Blake as he turned around.

"This is not acceptable." She made her voice calm and unemotional as she could. "You might be used to having everything your way, but not this time, not with me."

He emptied his drink, placed the glass down, and moved so suddenly his hands were on her shoulders locking her in place, before she could blink. He lowered his face to hers.

"I am going to have everything my way, Dakota." There was a hint of lust in the way he pronounced her name that sent a shiver down her spine. "When it comes to business, I am calling the shots until the conference ends. The sooner you learn that the better for both of us."

Their gazes did battle, but if he thought she would back down, he would be doomed to disappointment. He released her, and they stood less than a foot from one another. When he reached out to stoke the back of his hand against her cheek, Dakota barely managed not to lean her face into the caress. Gritting her teeth, she spoke, "I will follow your lead in all matters pertaining to this investigation. But this is my hotel room, and you are not welcome here."

"Each time we kissed I didn't force that sweet tongue of yours into my mouth or the moan from your throat." His voice was husky as he removed his cufflinks. "Are you positive I'm not welcome?"

Dakota broke eye contact and regretted it as she forced her gaze off his smooth muscled torso. Desire re-ignited and a warm flush spread from her neck to her cheeks. Truth was the cornerstone of her profession. She lived by it; strove to find and write about the truth. But at the moment what she wanted more than anything else was to lie.

She smiled coolly. "Very."

"One last chance to change your mind."

"Are you so arrogant you think after one kiss I'd let you into my bed?"

"I planned on more kissing before we made it to the bed."

She closed her eyes and let out a sigh of impatience. It seemed that men, no matter their age and status, still acted like boys. She turned away and began to walk toward the bedroom. "Go to bed, Blake."

"Go change into something more comfortable, Dakota," he grinned.

His comment had the desired effect, and he watched her nice backside until she walked into the master suite and slammed the door. And that was exactly what he wanted.

Taking advantage of her absence, he went over to her purse, and after a glance to assure himself he was still alone, reached into his pocket and withdrew a micro sized high-powered tracking device. Attaching it to the underside of the zippered pocket, he checked to ensure it was secure, then set her purse back in place. As long as she was aware he could be listening to her calls, she would not use her mobile phone or the hotel phone. Any move she made to contact the senator or to meet with him would be outside of his presence. Too much was at stake to let her roam free. He needed to know where she was at all times.

After he finished checking his handiwork, Blake grinned and took a seat on the sofa. When the door to the bedroom opened and Dakota walked into the room, every organ in his body seized.

His gaze trailed upward from her burgundy-colored toes, caressed the brown slender legs, strolled past the white terry cloth robe and stopped on her face. Her face devoid of makeup, if possible, was more beautiful than before. She'd also brushed her hair. Freed from its bindings, the midnight tresses flowed down her back and made her eyes all the more alluring. He searched for the one word to describe her at that exact moment, and the only one that came to his mind was temptress.

He stood and walked over to her. Without asking, he reached out and hooked one of her curls under his finger. The silken strands felt even better than they looked. He brought it to his nose and inhaled the clean flowery scent. "If I didn't know you, I would have thought by your performance tonight you'd been born into the diplomatic culture."

"Since you don't know me that well, how do you know I wasn't?"

"Dakota Montgomery. Twenty-nine year old African- and Native-American female. Born and raised as an only child in North Dakota. Graduated from high school with honors. Top of class at Princeton University, masters degree in Journalism from Columbia University. You spent over a year doing research in Vietnam, signed up as a foreign correspondent covering the Middle East and Africa."

"You're good."

"I like to know as much as I can about things I'm interested in." Blake only mentioned the highlight of her report. All the details remained unread in a folder nestled inside his briefcase.

Awareness flickered in her eyes, but her tone was still nonchalant when she answered. "Maybe you should have been the journalist, because I've had a very difficult time trying to dig up information on you, Blake Holland."

"You could ask."

Her lips inched upward at his response. "People, no matter their intentions, have a tendency to not tell the full truth."

"People lie," he translated.

"A high percentage of the time. But the facts and the evidence never lie."

Their words hung in the air between them, took on a deeper meaning. Currents of tension thrummed between them. Dakota tugged her hand, but he didn't let go of them. His eyes darkened with a look she'd seen before but couldn't readily classify. Her stomach abruptly hollowed when she identified his expression.

Lust. Raw and powerful, it stilled her heart for an instant before driving it to an accelerated pace. She recognized the hunger on his face. She was less acquainted with the answering desire it evoked. Passion leapt and threatened to break free as the world as she had known it tilted on its axis, and all she could do was helplessly watch as his mouth came crashing down on hers. His hand released hers and slid around her waist. Moving her head, she repositioned her mouth, deepening the kiss. When he urged her closer, she leaned in willingly, instinctually, until they were locked against each other.

There were a few moments when they lazily sampled each other that Dakota felt her control return. She'd pull back in a minute, she told herself. As soon as she'd sated her curiosity of the irresistible confidence he wore like a cloak.

Blake's tongue probed deeper into her mouth in a velvet glide. He was a man who knew how to kiss a woman, she acknowledged. Deep and hot, wet and long, branding his possession. Slow one instant and fast and rough the next, as if in the next second he would rip away her clothing and plunge into her hard.

That thought made her rein in her hormones. They shared neither trust nor friendship. She only knew of him via second hand information and background reports. She dragged her lips from his, stiffened and tried to move away from him.

His mouth went to her neck, and his teeth scored the cord there. A shudder ran through her body and weakened her knees to the point Dakota had to grab on to his shoulders for the fear she would fall. The flimsy fabric of the silk kimono was pushed upward to allow his hand to slide up her leg and cup her bottom. Breathing heavily, she opened her mouth to tell him to stop, but his mouth settled on her again for a carnal kiss, explicit of things to come. When he pulled away, her arms fell to her side and she hugged them close to her chest. Nerves were still bumping in her veins, Dakota took a step back. "Get out, Blake."

"Are you sure you want to go to bed alone tonight?" His tone was practically condescending.

She stared, stunned at the man's arrogance. Anger roared in her head and made her ears ring. "You pompous, overpaid, stupid jerk," Dakota spit. "Maybe...maybe for a split second I thought you were human, but I won't make that mistake again. If you want a bedmate, call your assistant."

Coolly stalking over to the hotel suite's connecting door, she opened it and stood back. "I like men with intelligence, charity, kindness, respect and honor."

"Like Peter O'Connor," he said mockingly.

Despite her intention not to be baited, Dakota responded, "Like Peter. I know he is a good man and he'd never betray his country. Just because you'd trade everything for money and power, doesn't mean everyone is just as mercenary."

His eyes flared with hostility as her words hit home. After he walked past her into his hotel room, Dakota slammed the door and locked it.

Bound by Moonlight

Later that night, Dakota knew it would be a sleepless night because she was so wound up. She had been caught off-guard by Nobu's offer. But that wasn't what was bothering her. She punched the pillow. Four hours had passed since Blake had first kissed her at the reception, and her body still burned with the memory of his lips on hers, his fingertips in her hair. The touch was electric, sending waves of desire throughout her body.

Whatever the outcome of the conference, there would be a reckoning between them, and it would be as raw as it would be unforgettable. Yet when it was all over and Peter was safe from harm, she'd walk away. She'd go to her next assignment and continue to expose the truth. She closed her eyes and tried to recall Peter's handsome face, but couldn't. Blake's arrogant visage stared back, and it was his ebony gaze that followed her into a restless sleep.

Chapter 8

D amn you, Blake Holland!" Dakota's voice accompanied the sound of a door slamming.

Without batting an eye, Blake ignored the threat of Dakota's impending arrival. He knew exactly why she was angry, and the thought would have brought a smile to his face had he not been irritated she hadn't told him of her intention to meet with Nobu.

Fresh from a hot shower, he'd just finished drying off and wrapping the towel around his hips when she stepped into the room.

"What the hell do you think you're doing?"

"Getting ready for work," he replied while patting his face with a steaming hot towel. Meeting her eyes in the mirror, he raised both his eyebrows. To underscore the point, he picked up his English shaving brush and applied a slick of shaving oil to his jaw, then spread on a layer of cream.

"You know what I mean. Why won't those marble statues you call diplomatic security agents let me leave my suite?"

He watched her raise her hands and shake them in his direction. His reaction to seeing her, catching the scent of her perfume as it wafted though the steam-filled bathroom, was instantaneous. A rush of blood shot through his veins, and his pulse increased its pace.

Her face blew him away every time. The first time he'd seen that beautiful face, his detached coolness had been ripped away. In the past, he'd always been the one in control of the relationship. It had been his decision when it began and when it ended. He'd planned meticulously, and he'd always worked his plan. He'd never allowed himself to get caught up in the emotional rollercoaster of being with one woman for an extended amount of time. His inability to consider Dakota Montgomery in a casual manner would soon drive him crazy, and his mind dwelled on it in the way a tongue prodded a sore tooth.

The outfit she wore, a pantsuit that emphasized her long slender legs and perfect bottom, was camel brown colored and blended well with her complexion. She was incredibly beautiful. There was no other way to describe her.

As Blake felt himself harden, he was thankful the thick towel would cover his physical response to her presence. It had been a long time since he'd been with a woman. After occupying himself with fashion models, socialites and rich divorcees, he'd gotten tired of the games. So for the past year he'd buried himself in his work, trying to ignore the every increasing dissatisfaction with his bachelor status.

The feminine scent of Dakota's perfume wafted into the room. The throb in his groin grew to an ache that told him he hadn't had sex in too long, and it was way past time for him to take care of that particular physical need. He'd been too busy with his new career, the intensive travel schedule and the difficulty of finding a woman who met his needs to look after that part of his life, but that was going to change. Dakota Montgomery, he decided, would be the one to change it.

Blake rinsed the shave brush, and then picked up his razor. "You can leave as long as you take one of them with you."

"I need to go somewhere alone."

"Not happening."

Blake heard what he thought was a growl before she continued, "What is it going to take to get it through your thick head that we're on the same side? You can trust me."

"I can trust you to look out for O'Connor, but what about my negotiations, Dakota? Nobu is only trying to find a way in, and he's going to try to use you to get to me."

Blake filled the sink halfway with water, and then positioned the blade for his first stroke. His eyes left hers and, with a surgeon's precision, carefully shaved with the grain.

Her eyes widened, and it was a moment before she could think of a response. Her first inclination was to slap him. But as soon as the tide of anger rose, it crashed against the shore of her logic. Taking a deep breath, Dakota stood straight and with her tone pitched to near freezing, she said, "You bugged me."

Blake finished with his right cheek and started on the left. "I didn't need to. I expected him to make a move on you. I didn't anticipate he would be so aggressive. He must feel the Japanese negotiating team is planning to make serious concessions on the raising import quota."

Seeing an opportunity, she pounced. "If he's truly desperate, then he can make a mistake. Let me meet him for breakfast, Blake. There's a chance I can gather useful information."

"No," he said, the word spoken strongly, his look compelling. He put down the razor, turned on the hot water and rinsed off the remaining dots of shaving cream. He grabbed a towel, patted his face and turned around. "I can't take that risk."

Dakota pressed her lips together, deciding for the moment to not say anything, trying not to let the sensations caused by the sight of his strong chest swamp her ability to think. "What can happen over breakfast at his office?"

"Nobu is not some meek Japanese businessman, trying to turn a profit, Dakota. He's the nephew of the Yamada clan's head boss. The man was sent to America to learn how to help launder money for the largest criminal organization in Japan. According to the latest report we've managed to get from the Japanese police, everyone who has gone against Nobu has disappeared or become one of his staunchest allies after an accidental death in their family."

"How can I help if you block me at every turn?" She'd meant for her words to come out strong. Instead, she sounded forlorn.

"I won't sacrifice your safety for O'Connor's, Dakota. You can't ask that of me."

Her jaw set. "It's my call, Blake. I'm a big girl. This is no different from my other assignments. You know I can handle it."

He took a step forward and trailed his fingertips over the soft curve of her cheek. "Maybe *you* can," he said softly, "but I can't take the risk of Nobu using you to get to me."

Bound by Moonlight

Her eyes dropped down and she nibbled on her bottom lip. If he didn't have a meeting to attend and breakfast waiting, Blake could have taken advantage of the enticing view and kissed her. Inhaling deeply, he fought down the urge to take her mouth and instead took her hand and squeezed. "We can discuss other options over breakfast. For now, I'll send someone downstairs to give Nobu your apologies."

"We could be making a mistake, Blake," Dakota warned as a last ditch effort to get him to change his mind.

"Warning duly noted. Now how about you go pour two cups of coffee while I get dressed?" He impulsively cupped her bottom and was rewarded with a furious glance. "Don't want to be late for your first meeting, do you? Very important person speaking, I hear."

When Dakota and Blake arrived at the embassy, the conference strategy meeting was already underway—the tension in the conference room was palpable. She took a seat in the back at a spare chair, pulled out her laptop and proceeded to ignore everyone in the room as a member of the team presented economic information he had gathered.

There was a slight pause as Blake took his seat at the table and began to review the briefing material. All the while, Dakota kept her eyes directed to the laptop, although she was well aware of the interest their late arrival had brought. She'd also detected an undertone of hostility in their eyes. It seemed that the new trade representative wasn't the only one who disliked journalists.

"Since the day of our arrival in Japan, there have been several inquires by the Japanese Ministry of International Trade for detailed product specifications from a number of American construction material companies." Blake paused to let the statement sink in. "They've also started a project to formally submit requests for proposals for the construction of a new nuclear facility in Hokkaido. So far, we've met these latest events as delay tactics. We are still planning to continue pressing for unilateral access to the Japanese market."

Blake cleared his throat. The room became silent. When he spoke, his deep voice resonated throughout the room.

"A few years ago, I was involved in the friendly take-over of a multi-national bank. When the heads of all the various banks gathered together to help strategize on how to go from the present situation to a stronger future situation, everyone had their own agenda and plan. It took weeks for the team to agree to simple unimportant things; it took months to agree on the new corporate structure. I'm not saying this to justify my job; I'm mentioning this because there is a good possibility we will have to leave something on the table during this conference. And I need all of you to work together in the interests of the American people to come up with what we can live with and what we can't. I need that analysis on my desk before noon tomorrow."

There were murmurs and sighs as the team around the table began to move around. Dakota sat back and put her fingers on the keyboard, but as she typed ever so often, she would glance upward and look at Blake.

He looked handsome as always, but she knew that if she stood close to him, she would see the tattletale signs of a restless night. The shad-owed circles under her eyes matched his own. She'd glimpsed them this morning as they shared a quick breakfast before departing for the embassy. Although she'd tried to subtly change his mind about her meeting with Nobu, he'd still been adamantly against the idea.

They both agreed it would be a shot in the dark, but at the moment Dakota really didn't care. All she wanted was to do *something*. By the end of the day, she would have completed her first full week in Tokyo, yet she had nothing to show for her efforts but a handful of theories.

"Dakota."

She looked over as Blake sat in the seat next to hers. Dakota kept her eyes locked on the computer screen thinking it would help, but it didn't. The scent of his cologne wafted to her nose, and her body's reaction was swift and uncontrollable as her breasts tingled. She blinked rapidly in the hope of clearing her thoughts, but all it did was remind her of the moment she'd stopped in the doorway of his bathroom.

If he'd taken that moment to look at her computer screen, all he could see was a jumble of words. Instead of seeing him dressed in the impressive suit, each time Dakota had looked up at him during the meeting, she'd mentally stripped him of his clothing. It should have been against the law for the man to have such a smooth, hard chest. The memory of Blake standing naked except for the thick white towel would forever remain etched in her mind as anxious desire strummed though her body. Mesmerized, her eyes had followed a droplet of water as it rolled down his back and disappeared into the small crevice leading to his perfect backside.

Dakota shifted, uncomfortable in her seat, and crossed her legs. Conscious their interaction was on camera and under the scrutiny of the other members of the trade delegation who remained in the conference room, Dakota managed to coolly turn her head and make eye contact. "Yes?"

His lips parting in a slow, sharp smile as she looked at him. "I'm going to need you to sit out of the room for the rest of the afternoon. We've set up a temporary office for you on another floor, and you should have access to public records, the Internet and a phone line. Agent Bradford over there," he waved at a skinny brown-haired man standing by the door, "will be your escort for the day. Keep in mind, this is just a procedural requirement due to your lack of security clearance. Please make sure he's with you at all times and that you don't happen to wander to other sections of the embassy."

His voice had increasingly taken on a condescending tone that grated against her nerves. Although she theorized most of his speech was a performance, it still bothered her. Drawing in a deep breath, Dakota clamped down on the sarcastic response she would have loved to say and instead smiled. "I understand."

"I've scheduled us to meet for dinner to discuss your interview schedule with the team. Is eight o'clock too late for you?"

Dakota began to gather her things and slid the laptop back in the bag. "That will be fine."

"Good." He shot her a deep meaningful look before standing and holding out a hand.

Evil man, Dakota thought. For a second she considered ignoring the gesture, and she let her eyes reflect that fact. Yet the challenging sparkle in Blake's eyes dared her to follow through. Gritting her teeth, she reached up and took his hand to stand. Just that small flesh-to-flesh contact stopped her breath. Although innocent, her mind took the moment and ran with it. Within the space of a few seconds, she'd thought imagined his caressing her body, his hands grasping her hips, and positioning her for his entry. Her eyes must have reflected her thoughts as Blake's nostrils flared and his gaze deepened.

"Thank you," she murmured.

"Anytime." His smile deepened with a secret humor.

Without another word, she picked up her bag and headed out of the room.

A few hours later, staring at the computer at her temporary desk, Dakota walked into Blake's office and sat down. Although she'd sworn to herself she would not get emotionally involved with any man until she resolved her feelings for Peter, she realized she had broken her oath. If she were brutally honest, she would confess that with what little she knew about Blake, it was foolish to care for him.

Most people revealed something about themselves in the course of conversation. From Blake there had been nothing. She recalled he had carefully directed the conversation while giving her the illusion of control. As soon as she answered one question or finished telling him about her travels and family, he'd ask another question. If she hadn't been caught up in seeing the warmth in his eyes and the smile on his lips; she might have caught on sooner.

Bound by Moonlight

The average person wasn't so secretive about himself or as skilled in obtaining information without sharing any, unless he had something to hide.

Deep in thought, she rubbed her brow and stared down at the perfectly organized desk. There was so much more going on with Blake than she ever thought. Many people of his stature held their privacy in high regard and guarded it zealously. But because of his position, Blake Holland invited public curiosity. Her cover story involved digging underneath his stony exterior and exposing the man underneath. But would she like what she found or would it expose a facet of Blake that should remain buried?

As a journalist, she'd learned long ago the truth didn't set a person free. Getting to the truth always had repercussions and not all of them are good. Ultimately, she would have to choose between doing her job and pretending to work on the article while being bait or following her conscience and warning Peter about the ongoing investigation.

Perhaps a better question, she mused reaching out and lifting a crystal paperweight and balancing it in the palm of her hand, was why couldn't she stop thinking about him?

Getting up from her chair, she strolled over to where Blake sat bent over the computer. "Everything okay?" she inquired, leaning over his shoulder.

Patience didn't come naturally to Dakota. Because it was crucial in her line of work, she'd made an effort to cultivate the trait. She'd once spent two weeks sequestered in a shack, waiting for an overly arrogant African warlord to grant her an interview. But somehow, with Blake Holland at her side, patience seemed even more elusive. The man made her nervous. She was too keyed to him for it to be otherwise.

He quickly switched to another screen. Keying in information, he pressed the enter key. "How good is your memory?"

"Excellent."

"Do you remember this man from the consulate party?"

The man with his dark eyes and tailor-made suit and flanked by bodyguards appeared on the screen. It didn't take long for her to recognize Takeda. She might not have remembered him from last night, but the photo helped her recall where she'd seen him. Hiroshi Takeda, he was the heir apparent to one of Japans largest corporations. "We spoke briefly last night."

"You spoke for approximately five minutes, before motioning to Nobu."

Her eyes widened, and it was a moment before she could think of a response. "You were watching them the entire time last night weren't you?"

"No. I anticipated he would do something like that. It's like chess. He wants to know where all the pieces are on the board. On paper Nobu and Takeda are competitors. In reality Takeda takes orders from Nobu. Last night was just a small display of their relationship. Nobu likes to manipulate people and you are his new target."

Some of her initial outrage dissipated, but she was still angry. "I am not a pawn," she barked.

His brow rose slightly and a smirk curled his lips. "Aren't you? You're here because of Peter. How does that make this situation of your own free will?"

Enraged by both the truth in his statement and the look on his face, Dakota pivoted on her high heels and strode out of the room.

Chapter 9

There was a time when journalists were given the respect and autonomy reserved for an elected member of government, but as Dakota sat in the consulate car that arrived for her outside the hotel and watched as it took her closer to dinner with Blake Holland, she reminded herself she was in a special situation where a positive outcome justified the means. She even tried to convince herself that anyone in her situation would do the same. But her somber mood did not lift. Earlier that morning when Peter had returned her phone call, Blake had stood next to her as she'd told him her assignment in Tokyo was to write an article on the trade conference. She'd lied to Peter, and there was nothing she could do to change it.

Shaking her head, she looked out the window, and her spirits lightened somewhat as she became aware of how much more alive the city seemed at night. In the distance, she could see the Tokyo Tower, all lit up, competing with the sunset, which overlooked the skyline. She looked down, and the sidewalks were filled with thousands of people and bright neon lights. Dakota had not seen a sight like it anywhere, not even Singapore or Hong Kong. Tokyo's ocean of buildings, streets, people and signs blended with the shadows and the resulting scene could have been a scene from a futuristic cartoon.

As soon as she passed through the entrance, Dakota stopped in her tracks. She'd dined in restaurants around the world, but this one seemed different. As the sliding doors retracted, revealing the garden like entrance of the restaurant's reception area, Dakota felt as if she were stepping into another world.

"Good evening, Montgomery-*san*," came a perfectly pitched female voice. Dakota shook her head and turned her attention to the kimono-clad hostess as the woman bowed to greet her. Dakota's eyes grew round, as the woman was a living breathing Japanese doll. Her jet-black hair was pulled back into a complex chignon held still by wooden combs; her complexion was the color of winter snow unbroken except by bright red lips and expertly drawn eyebrows. Her kimono could have been a painting with its intricate cranes, flowers, and designs.

"Montgomery-*san*," the hostess repeated her name with a slight up pitch of a question

Dakota shook her head, embarrassed to be caught gawking like a tourist. "Yes."

"If you would please change into the slippers, I will take you to the dining room."

She looked down, and sure enough, a single pair of sandals waited. Slipping out of her high heels, she slid her feet into the sandals and stepped up onto the tatami mat.

"Has Mr. Howard already arrived?"

"A mere ten minutes before your arrival. I would not worry. It is always a good tactic to keep a gentleman waiting."

She smiled and nodded. "I couldn't agree with you more."

Before they left the room, Dakota stopped and pointed to a magnificent piece of glass-encased cloth on the wall of the entry foyer.

"May I ask where I would purchase that piece? My father would love it."

The hostess smiled and shook her head. "I am sorry, but it is a family heirloom. The owner's grandmother fashioned it from an old obi sash."

After a short walk around an open courtyard, they stopped at an invisible doorway. The hostess slid back the shoji screen. Dakota's pulse began to race at the sight of Blake seated on cushions. Following the hostess's direction, she stepped into the private room, and the sound of the door sliding closed seemed to fill the space. A single cushion sat in front of a table fitted with a deep well that allowed legs to stretch comfortably to the floor.

"Please have a seat. I don't bite."

Damn, she silently cursed. As she walked toward him, Dakota couldn't seem to focus on anything else, and although soft music played in the background, all she could hear was the beating of her heart. Dakota felt a bit awkward as she lowered herself onto the pillow opposite Blake. She hadn't anticipated being completely alone with him. She'd assumed they'd dine in a main dining area, yet this small intimate private dining room was too intimate. The lack of distractions combined with the relaxed confidence he exuded was more seductively powerful than any aphrodisiac she'd come across in her travels.

"You look very nice, Dakota."

"Thank you," she picked up her napkin and used it as a shield until she could marshal her runaway thoughts. "Will it just be you and me tonight?"

"That shouldn't surprise you. It's been just us since the first night we met."

She placed the menu down and adjusted her legs to a more comfortable position. "Look, Blake, despite what happened last night, I can't get involved with you."

"Can't or won't?"

"Does it make a difference?"

"You know it does."

"Fine, I won't get involved with you."

"Because of Senator O'Connor? I've heard rumors there is more than meets the eyes with your friendship.

Dakota didn't resist the urge to let out a rude snort. "What is it with you men? If a woman doesn't want to sleep with you, it can't be because of you; it has to be another man."

"Isn't it?"

Even though she wanted to look away, Dakota maintained eye contact. "My relationship with Peter is none of your business."

His hand struck out like a snake and clamped on to her wrist. "The second you responded to my kiss, it became my business. Now answer my question, and I warn you I will know if you're lying to me."

The breath stilled in her lungs at the heavy intensity of his stare. "Strictly platonic."

"By whose wishes?"

"Peter's," she said bitterly.

His hand disappeared, and Dakota savored a very hollow victory as she continued her story. "I was seventeen and fancied myself in love with him for over a year. How could I have not thought I wasn't in love with Peter? My family adored him, he was outgoing, charming, handsome, caring and wounded. In retrospect, that's what drew me to him. We spent hours together out riding, talking and fishing.

"I wanted to prove that Peter returned my affection, so when my father left us alone at the ranch for a weekend, I snuck into Peter's room."

Her gaze focused inward and she relived the moment as she retold the most humiliating moment of her life.

"Dakota, what are you doing in my bed?" The absolute look of astonishment on Peter's face should have been adequate warning, but she'd been determined.

"I'm waiting for you, of course," she said with all the maturity her teenage voice could muster.

"Are you all right?" He took a few steps into the bedroom. Her eyes, which had been locked on his face, moved south and her throat went dry. It wasn't like she hadn't seen Peter in a towel before. They shared the same bathroom. But this was way different. His reddish brown hair was all spiky and his brown colored chest hair was still damp from the shower. He even had a different scent. A masculine scent.

She cleared her throat and ran her tongue over her lips to moisten them before replying. "I'm fine."

"Then why are you in my room, and why do I smell perfume, little bit?" Color flamed Dakota's cheeks as she reached to his statement. Peter just stood staring down at her as if she'd grown another head.

Dakota ran her fingers through her hair and narrowed her eyes like she'd seen a million times in the movies. It wasn't supposed to be that way. He was supposed to take one look and be overcome with desire.

She sat on the bed, and in the romance novels she'd read, the scene called for her to be naked, but she hadn't managed to get over her own self-consciousness, so she'd gone through her mother's lingerie drawers. The black negligee covered her body, barely. She sat up on her knees, careful to maintain eye contact. "I want you to make me into a woman, Peter. Your woman."

"God, Dakota, do you know what you're asking?" He sat on the edge of the bed.

Nervous, almost jumping out of her skin, Dakota couldn't even reach out and touch him. Instead, she swung her legs onto the side of the bed and sat next to Peter. "Yes. I love you, and I want to give myself to you."

"Did you get that out of the trashy romance novels I've seen you with this last month?"

Dakota looked over and hated to admit that the uncontrollable passion he'd have for her she'd read about in the books hadn't happened. He seemed to be having a very easy time of keeping his hands off her. Maybe she was too skinny, or she should have left her hair up, maybe put on more lipstick.

"I asked you a question, Dakota."

His sharp tone brought her gaze back to his face. "No," she snapped.

Peter's brows rose, and his green eyes held a mocking twinkle.

Dakota took an exasperated breath. "Okay, maybe a little, but I've been in love with you since the first summer you came home with Dad."

"Wow, I'm honored you have a crush on me. But I can't return your feelings."

At that moment, Dakota thought her heart would burst as wave after wave of misery flooded her soul. Tears rushed to her eyes, and she dashed them away. "Why can't you love me? Am I that hideous?"

"No...No." He moved to take her hand, but she pulled away and stood up.

"Stop lying," she whispered through a clogged throat.

"That's one of the things we never do to one another, Dakota. I will always tell you the truth. You are a beautiful girl, and you will grow up to be a beautiful woman, and you will make some man incredibly blessed. But I cannot be that man."

"Because of my father?" she asked. .

He smiled a slow sad smile. "Because, little bit. I love you like a sister."

Sometime during her story a server had entered, filled her wine glass and placed an arrangement of savory hors d'oeuvres displayed on a gilded bamboo on the table. She shook her head and reached for her chopsticks. As much she could, Dakota tried to keep her voice cool. "So there you have it. Any questions?"

"What does he mean to you now?"

Dakota retrieved her chopsticks as she pondered an answer to his question. "Mean?"

"Don't be coy, Dakota. It's not your style. Just answer the question."

Dakota met his dark stare. "He's still Peter to me, Blake. He's still the boy my father brought home when I was fifteen. Still the person I would trust with my life."

"But…"

She sighed and would have slumped in her chair had she not been sitting on a backless pillow. "I've long since realized I had a girlhood crush."

Saying the words aloud also allowed Dakota the chance to admit to herself that it was safer to live in the fantasy of what would never be than risk falling in love with someone and having her soul mate die like her mother had died on her father."

"It seems Peter has managed to do something I don't think I ever could," Blake said huskily.

Very aware of the heat in his eyes and their closeness, Dakota dared to ask. "And what's that?"

"Not making love to you when he had the chance. If you choose to show up in my bed wearing a black negligee, rest assured, you won't be leaving the bed."

Heat suffused her cheeks and Dakota reached out to pick up her wine glass in the anticipation of relieving her suddenly dry throat. "It's a good thing that won't happen."

"There's always my dreams, of course. I'd like to propose a toast: to our new friendship." Blake lifted his glass.

"I'll toast to that," she replied. Dakota squashed a hysterical giggle. Everything about her life since meeting Blake Holland was surreal. And

79

Bound by Moonlight

now she'd told the man about Peter. Incredulous by her own actions, she clicked her glass against his, then took a deep swallow. The velvety, almost sweet fruity flavor of the plum wine sent a wave of pleased relaxation through her body.

"Now that we have the heavy stuff out of the way, enjoy the food. This is only the beginning."

"The beginning of what?"

"One of the best seven course meals you've had in your life."

A few moments later as they both ate, Dakota tried not to stare. Not that she hadn't seen men eat, but this was different. Watching him savor his food and lick the tip of his chopsticks was having a surprisingly arousing effect on her. She knew he would be the same in bed. Blake wasn't a ten-minute man; he would make love for hours. An involuntary shudder of heat ran up and down her spine.

"Did the driver find the restaurant okay?"

"Yes. Although I had my doubts we would get here alive. Just because the streets are narrower, doesn't mean the man needed to drive faster. At one point, I closed my eyes and prayed."

He threw his head back and laughed. Right then and there, she decided Blake's laugh was lethal. It filled her skin and made her feel warm and fuzzy. Dakota relaxed. "I wouldn't have believed Japanese drivers could be so aggressive."

"Tokyoites could give the Italians a run for their money. If you think about it, it makes perfect sense, seeing that all of the hi-tech video games are based on actual city streets, and many of the drivers play them at home."

"That doesn't make me feel any better." Her smile matched his.

"I'll make sure the driver sticks to the speed limit on our way back to the hotel."

"That would be very welcome. I would hate to have this wonderful meal find itself on your shoes."

"You're just not a city girl are you, Dakota?"

"I am not, and you know this because you read my file. I also know your hometown in West Virginia is a long way from urban. Just like you,

80

I spent half my childhood in a city with one store, one gas station, one traffic light, and five churches."

His eyes held hers, displaying a warmth that challenged her to respond in kind.

That devastating grin of his was back in full effect. Without a doubt, the up tilt of his generous lips and perfect white teeth would appear in her fantasies for a few nights. What was it about Blake that made her want to throw caution into the winds and forget about Peter and the trade conference and just delve into more personal investigation as to what Blake Holland looked like naked in bed? How could someone she hadn't known more than a week manage to hold such a physical and mental attraction?

Dakota lifted the bowl of miso soup to her mouth as she sipped the liquid. She met Blake's eyes. Before she left Japan, they would know each other in a very Biblical sense. She knew that like she knew her own name. When they were close, her body reacted. Hidden underneath her padded bra, her nipples were hard and sensitive. The apex of her thighs throbbed and begged to be filled. Even her mouth longed to taste his skin. The question was how would she handle what happened next?

Later that evening after indulging in an almost three hour meal, Dakota paused outside of her hotel suite. "Thank you for a dinner."

Blake stood close. Too close. So close all she needed to do was tilt her head up and their lips would touch.

His voice was melodic. "It doesn't have to end you know."

"Yes, it does." She slowly shook her head from side to side. "I don't think that would be a good idea. Remember, we're keeping our relationship strictly professional."

"I don't remember making that agreement." He stepped back and smiled. "Besides, I think we've already crossed that line."

Dakota's brows knitted with confusion. "When?"

"When you went from my daytime fantasies to my midnight dreams and started keeping me up all night and taking cold showers. Sleep well tonight, we've got a busy day tomorrow."

Bound by Moonlight

She stared at his back as he walked to the door of his hotel suite. Sparing one last glance at the diplomatic service agent standing in the hallway, she pushed in her hotel keycard. Dakota was glad when the door closed. At least for the next couple of hours life would make sense.

For the second night in a row, Dakota tossed fitfully in her queen-size bed. Every time she closed her eyes, she thought of him. *Blake*. She saw his darkly handsome face when she closed her eyes. His mystifying brown eyes…strong jaw, his arrogant grin…lips so sensuous…oohh and so firm.

Her brown hand clutched the soft pillow under her head…as she remembered the way his mouth had felt on hers. How gently he kissed her, nibbling at her like she was a delectable dessert…then dipping his tongue inside her mouth and lapping up every single inch like it was the sweetest taste he'd ever tasted. A soft moan escaped her lips as she rolled over again and pushed down the comforter. "Blake, why are you torturing me?" she whispered in the darkness.

"I've been asking myself that same question."

Dakota opened her eyes. She spotted him immediately in the shadows just beyond her open window. A lazy grin was on his face when he stepped from the shadows toward her. His gaze flicked down her uncovered body and she could practically feel the heat from his eyes as they rested on her naked breast.

"Let me in, sweetheart" he groaned, moving swiftly toward her, his hand resting on her smooth mocha colored cheek. "Let me love you."

Instinctively, she rubbed her cheek against his palm, enjoying the warmth of his fingers. He traced his fingertips along the smooth contours of her face…caressing her lovely high forehead, the corners of her exotically shaped eyes, her upturned nose…the hallows of her cheeks and finally the delicate bow shape of her mouth.

"Exquisite," he whispered, his finger lingering on the supple, sensitive bottom lip. Her tongue darted out in temptation.

"Witch," he groaned, as he bent and sought to taste her lips with his own.

Immediately her mouth opened for him, and his tongue surged inside. Tasting, licking and sucking her sweet mouth in delight. His hands wound tightly in her lustrous hair as he kissed her with a fervor that surprised even him. Her hands moved to his shoulders where they began a feverish exploration of his body. This was erotic. Kissing her while she lay naked and he still fully dressed in slacks and a shirt. He still had on his shoes, she thought wildly. Inside his pants his manhood sprang to life as her tongue stroked his while her hands slid under his shirt, to meet his hot flesh.

As his tongue dipped in her mouth, his fingers slipped between her parted thighs. She was soaking wet, he discovered delightfully as his fingers deftly caressed the swollen feminine flesh, parting the way to reach the heated satiny texture within.

Dakota's breath came fast as her mouth tore from his, and her head arched back as she released moan after moan as he fingers worked inside her. Blake glided out of the wet passage, to seek the tiny supersensitive nub of flesh as her moans grew louder and her head rolled from side to side in rhythm with her hips as he stroked her.

It was her hands that deftly undid his button and zipper...her fingers gliding down the hard proof of his need as she unzipped his jeans. He moved away from her to strip off his remaining clothes and shoes, allowing her the fleeting pleasure of viewing his glorious body.

The pure lust she saw in his handsome features when he stared at her naked body made her drop back on the bed and pull him atop her her.

He had to get inside her or she would explode, Dakota thought. She was so hot and ready she had soaked his fingers. She gave a muffled cry of protest when his fingers left her. Somehow his erection jerked as it found the heated entrance on its own accord.

She was so tight, and he felt so good...she thought, and he wasn't even all the way in yet. "Please, Blake," she cried, brokenly. It was then that he surged up inside her, sliding deep up into her slippery silken heat, which clutched him instantly inside. Dakota looked up at the man who filled her so completely with surprise on her face. She'd had no idea how big and thick he was until he had thrust into her.

Bound by Moonlight

She had no idea he would be this good...She felt him pull out and begin to teasingly brush against her swollen clit sending her pulse racing erratically. Then when she thought she could bear no more of that sweet torture, he pushed himself deep inside her unbelievable wetness and began to buck wildly when her hips met his head on.

"So good," she moaned between breathless gasps.

"Come for me," he crooned in her ear, and he thrust harder and harder into her. She let out a soft mewl as she started to quiver.

Dakota could feel the pressure building up inside her, struggled to calm it but it was impossible. And as she gasped and her body shuddered with release, her eyes sprang open and she sat up in bed, throwing the comforter aside. The bedcovers were in complete disarray and heated skin was slick with perspiration.

A dream, her mind concluded.

This had to stop. She'd dreamed of him for the past few nights and repressed the memories as just the fantasies of a woman who had been alone and abstinent for far too long. But now she was wide-awake and her body practically screamed for his touch.

Taking a deep breath, she got up and went to the bathroom. What she needed was a good long shower.

Chapter 10

Senator Peter O'Conner gave up on the idea of sleep, switched on the lamp beside the table and sat up in his king-sized bed. Moonlight streamed in from the open curtains, and occasionally the sound of a large delivery trunk would rumble down the street. Washington, D.C. didn't sleep and neither did he. Peter looked at the blue binder that sat on the nightstand and moved to pick it up. He didn't really need to open it, because he knew its contents. Every picture, every translated word was etched into his consciousness. He had a child. A son who didn't carry his name. A boy he hadn't known existed until twenty-four hours ago.

Peter rubbed his brow and thought about all of his hopes and dreams. Everything he'd done in his life had been for his family. Including his application to West Point and subsequent promotion to captain in the Air Force. The only time he'd ever broken the rules was with Akiko. He thought about her behavior before he'd been transferred to Germany. Every word and tear took on a new meaning. Had she known about the child before he'd left? Had her parents forbidden her to talk to him? What had become of her life and the child's? Had she been ostracized for having his child? Guilt slammed into his chest. Had he known, he would have married her and brought her home. Now he was counted among the most powerful men in America, yet he lay in his bed alone. His mother and father long since buried. All he had was the O'Connor name, and that was of cold comfort.

Peter wanted to concentrate on what he could do to rectify the situation instead of concentrating on a past he couldn't change. Yet found himself wondering what kind of woman Akiko had become, would she still have feelings for him or would they have turned to hate. Flipping open the folder, he stared down at the formal picture of Akiko dressed in

Bound by Moonlight

an elegant Japanese kimono while his son, Daichi, wore a traditional school uniform consisting of a white dress shirt, necktie, blazer with school crest and dress trousers. When he looked into his son's face, his heart filled with pride. The little boy had his mother's eyes, but Peter could see traces of his father in both his features and the curly brown hair.

Peter looked at the clock on the bedside table, then went to pick up the telephone. He needed to prepare his friends and family for the news. He especially needed to brief his senior-level staff. The political fallout of his constituents discovering he'd had a child out of wedlock with an underage Japanese girl might cost him his career.

Before he could dial the number, the cell phone rang. Peter's brows furrowed as he looked at the caller ID, and then at the alarm clock. It was 2:54 A.M. Hardwick had only arrived in Tokyo the previous morning, and Peter hadn't expected him to call with a report until sometime later in the day. His pulse jumped as his mind ran through all kinds of reasons as to why the hired mercenary was reporting in so early. Taking a steadying breath, he opened the mobile phone and put it up to his ear.

"Senator, I apologize for the hour."

"No need. Do you have news about my son?"

"My local contacts have managed to tap into a few of the lower level members of Nobu's organization. He appears to be keeping the operation contained to a select few. We're getting reports that a few of his trusted employees have left the city and have been in Okinawa for the last two weeks. This would be about the time Ms. Nakamura and her son disappeared from her family's house. If everything goes according to plan and the informants credential's check out, we'll have them within the week."

For several heartbeats, Peter was silent, soaking up every word. When he responded, his voice held a rough edge of weariness. "It is imperative that you get to them before the conference, Hardwick."

"Yes, sir. I understand, and the team will do their best. The next step is where I take the woman and the boy after we locate them. I assume you want them out of the country?"

86

Peter rubbed his tired eyes as his mind worked on picking a safe location to hide them. He couldn't bring them to the States. Not only would that be the first place Nobu would look, but he also had to minimize the impact the scandal would have to his upcoming re-election bid.

Akiko, who'd never traveled far from Japan, had always spoken of traveling to England. It had been one of the numerous things about her he'd fallen in love with as a jaded solider. Her innocence and passion for people and culture not her own. He cursed himself for the situation he found himself in, and he cursed her as well for not telling him she was pregnant. "I have a friend with a flat in Knightsbridge. I'll forward you the address. Is there anything else you need?"

"No, sir. We'll go by a sea, land and air exit route. I recommend we avoid contact until the assignment is complete. Once we take the boy and his mother, they'll go after the woman."

Peter nodded. The idea had occurred to him, the second he'd learned of Dakota's assignment to cover the trade conference. His relationship with the Montgomery family was well known in his political circles and amongst his enemies. He and Dakota had always been close to one another. So close that during his run for election to the Senate, his opponent had publicly hinted that Peter and Dakota were lovers.

He'd watched her blossom from a pretty girl into a beautiful woman who'd developed a crush on him. Peter would have been a fool to deny he'd been aware of the transformation, but his respect for her father and his genuine love for Dakota had kept him from crossing the line. "She needs to be protected at all costs."

"She is already very secure. According to my sources, she's going to be under the watch of Representative Holland's security detail."

"I still want one of your men on her. If things get hot, I want her on the transport with Akiko and my son, understand?"

"This is going to add to the cost."

Peter rubbed his brow and sat back. The rock in his stomach hadn't moved since the day Howard approached him with the envelope. "I have plenty of money, Patrick, but what I don't have is time. Do what you have to do, bribe who you have to bribe, just get me my son."

Bound by Moonlight

"I'll update you before the end of the day."

"Thank you." Peter hung up the phone and stared ahead. His planning had only just begun. Before the month was over, he would carry two more titles in addition to Senator: father and husband.

Chapter 11

The next evening after dinner with the trade team, Dakota would have loved to have gone back to the hotel and immerse herself in a relaxing tub of hot water. But she had an appearance to make, and thus she was out on the town with Blake. Guided by the firm hand on the small of her back, she walked through the spacious entrance lobby and foyer toward the open doors leading into what she'd been told was one of the acoustical masterpieces of the world. Despite its exclusivity, or perhaps because of it, the concert hall was crowded.

She didn't find that hard to believe since the stainless steel exterior of the concert hall gave her the impression of the structure being more of a sculpture than of a building. Located in Ginza, the heart of Tokyo's upscale fashion and jewelry trade, the locale would play host to one of the highly talked groups of traditional Japanese drummers.

Before Blake could hand the attendant their ticket, she heard her name.

"Dakota, what are you doing here?"

She turned to see Anne Dumont, a financial journalist and former journalism school classmate. With her was Ivan Duntrof, a reporter for CNN in Japan.

"I've got to make a few phone calls, I'll meet you in the box," Blake murmured.

"Too late," she muttered. There was a hint of dry humor in her response. Plastering a smile on her face, she stepped away from Blake and played nice with her former rival.

"Good evening, Anne, Ivan. I'd like you to meet—"

"Blake Holland," Anne finished and greeted Blake with a kiss on the cheek. Normally Dakota didn't consider herself a jealous person, but that sight sent a wave of resentment snaking through her body.

Bound by Moonlight

Dressed perfectly in tailored evening clothes, the combination of Blake's close-shaven head, smooth jaw, straight nose, full lips and dark compelling eyes were downright lethal. Standing next to him while looking at Ivan and Anne made Dakota very aware of his sex appeal. And the woman in her saw red at Anne's come-back-to-my-bedroom smile.

Taking control of her thoughts and reminding herself she didn't care who Blake spent his time with because it was none of her business, Dakota smiled and held out a hand to Ivan. "You look well. I take it Tokyo has been treating you well?"

"It's great until I have to go up north to Hokkaido. Never been to a more brutally cold place in my life."

"So, Dakota, have you given up your ideals or is this a personal visit?" Anne asked. "I'd heard the normal rumors that you were in town, but I couldn't imagine why until now."

Like a shark with blood in the water, her college rival was fishing for a story. "Anne, if you really must know. I'm here on business."

"Do tell or is it secret?"

Dakota spared a short glance in Blake's direction. Seeing the muscle tick in his jaw tempted her to say something wicked, but she stuck with their cover story. "I'm working on writing a more personal piece on the trade conference."

"And I'm the lucky man who gets to help Dakota and make sure everything comes off without a hitch." Blake grinned.

Both reporters' attention swung to Blake. "How is it that the leader of the trade team gets assigned to help a journalist write a story?" Ivan asked suspiciously.

Dakota winked at them and allowed a trickle of laughter to escape her lips. "I wondered the same thing when I got the phone call. There are hundreds of better-qualified writers for this assignment. I was told that a certain incoming trade representative was an admirer of my work."

Lips quirked with mischief, Dakota slid a sideways glance at Blake. "As far as I can tell since I've been here, the representative has an appreciation for things outside of my field of professional expertise."

90

Just then the lights dimmed and rose, signaling the concert would soon start. Blake cleared his throat loudly, and the hand that had once rested gently on her back, gripped her arm.

Dakota bit back a sigh of relief and said, "I'm sorry but we really have to run. Our seats are on the other side of the room, and we don't want to appear like rude Americans."

"Of course." Anne nodded her head. "We'll catch up later."

"It was a pleasure meeting you." Blake's smile could have melted the polar icecaps, and Anne fell for it hook, line and sinker.

"I'll see you later," Dakota responded with a dazzling, smug smile. They both knew how the game would play out. Anne would call all of her contacts to verify Blake's story, and then the woman would beat down her door for information.

"Call me," Dakota tossed over her shoulder as Blake practically dragged her into the main auditorium and up the stairs to the semi-private booths.

"What the hell kind of game were you playing back there?"

Dakota stared at his impassive expression. "Oh, that. Just a little professional catfight. Nothing to worry about."

He sat her down, put a finger under her chin, then turned her face to his. The overhead halogen lights illuminated the sprinkling of white in his close-cropped hair, and she wondered what he would look like if he let his hair grow.

His lids lowered over his expressive eyes as he flashed the sensual smile that always sent sensual shivers up and down her spine. "Somehow I think it's more than a little catfight, Dakota."

Her eyes widened. "Really?"

The sound of her sultry voice floated around Blake like morning mist, drawing him in and seducing him with its hypnotic timbre. Every moment they spent together made him want to be with her more.

She challenged him at every turn. And when he thought he understood her, she changed. Before tonight, he couldn't gauge how she felt about him, but the scene he'd just witnessed gave him all the proof he needed. Tonight, Dakota's body and her mind had been on one accord.

Looking down, he stared at their entwined hands and for the first time noticed the difference in their coloring. Both were brown—hers amber, his burnished mahogany. Her fingers were long and slender—the hands of a pianist whose touch made him very aware of how much he would like to feel them on his skin. And what he did not want to admit was that her touch was something he'd come to crave more than anything in his life.

He sat back in his seat and released her hand. "I think you were jealous."

At the sound of her harsh indrawn breath, he braced himself for a furious denial. Instead, several moment of silence passed. Curious he looked over to see Dakota toying with her purse strap. "What? Cat got your tongue?"

"No," she replied with a lower tone. "But I wish he'd grabbed yours and ripped it to shreds."

"Bloodthirsty tonight, aren't you?"

"Only because I've spent the entire day being stonewalled and treated like a leper by your staff. I didn't know the anal retentive gene had to be present in all members of the trade staff."

"They're just doing their jobs," he defended his team at the same time Blake made a mental note to speak with them individually.

"And I should be doing mine instead of this bogus wait-and-see game."

She turned those pleading brown eyes on him, and Blake had an image of his little sister. All the protective instincts he in the past only had for his little sister, suddenly centered on the woman by his side. "Just be patient a little longer."

"What if Peter doesn't contact me, Blake? You could have gone though this elaborate set up for nothing."

"This won't be for nothing. Since the beginning of this investigation, we've uncovered more leaks and security holes than we'd ever imagined."

"Why won't you just let me ask him about Nobu, Blake? You can be in the room."

92

Angela Weaver

"Didn't you tell me you promised never to lie to Peter?"

She nodded slowly, and he pressed his point home. "Would you be willing to lie to him now? He's going to want to know why you're asking questions, and you can't tell him the truth."

Dakota withdrew as far as she could from him. Blake wanted to see her face, but the lights lowered and the master of ceremonies, dressed in traditional Japanese formal attire, took center stage. Within moments all conversation ceased as a screen retracted revealing Kodo, one of the elite taiko drumming groups in Japan.

Fourteen drummers clad in sweatbands and loincloths stood and took their positions around the massive drums. When they began, Blake lost all thought as waves of percussive sound seemed to turn the concert hall into a living heartbeat.

Everything disappeared when Dakota closed her eyes to the drumming. Her consciousnesses mixed with the primal power and beauty of the music. Somehow, it moved deadly aggression with utter tranquility. Their sound stretched from the lightest of rainfall to cataclysmic thunderclaps, from pleasant laughter to discordant fear and from silence to a wall of sound that transported her to a room. A bedroom. And in that space, Dakota created in her mind, there was just him. Blake, touching her naked body. There was no softness in him. No mercy. And his kiss was raw, unrestrained. His hands seemed to run over her skin. He grabbed her hair as his mouth ate hers, as if he wanted to feed on her. As if he would satiate himself with her kiss.

And as good as he gave, Dakota gave it all back. Her fingernails ripped into his back. Her tongue eagerly mated with his, sucking at his tongue; biting at his lip like an animal in heat. She pushed her pelvis against his. And the hard smoothness of his erection against her curls made her even hotter.

Always in the background, her body felt the pounding vibrations of the drums. And between one breath and the next one beat and the next; she let out a scream as he entered her in one stoke. His hand cupped her butt cheeks and he pushed her neck against the wall. He pushed against her and Dakota buried her face in his neck and bit him. As his pace

93

increased and she lifted her head as every muscle in her body began to tense and her nerves tingled with the approach of climax; and between one breath and the next, Blake disappeared and left her body screaming for completion. The world seemed to have grown silent, and she was crushed by the absence, crushed by the power of his loss, defeated by the complete silence as if life had stopped in an instant, not even a breath.

"Dakota?"

She jumped and would have stood up had if not for the hand on her arms.

"Sorry to wake you."

"I wasn't asleep," she whispered and struggled to catch her breath.

"I know."

She looked but it took her a moment to realize the import of his statement. Her eyes moved downward to find Blake's hand underneath her skirt. His finger had found the small space between her stockings and garters to move aside the elastic band of her panties. Her body shuddered again, and she grabbed a hold of the armrests to keep from bucking as his finger pressed against her clitoris.

"Who was it in your fantasy, Dakota?" he whispered in her ear.

Her face flushed with embarrassment, and she looked around wildly.

He stroked her not so gently and repeated his question. "Who was it in your fantasy, Dakota?"

"Who said you can touch me?" Dakota asked. She'd meant for the words to be hard and accusatory; instead her voice was soft and more of a whimper.

"You did. You grabbed my hand."

"I..." The emphatic denial died on her lips.

The pressure against her increased, and Dakota almost screamed at the intense pleasure.

"Who was it? And don't lie to me, because I will know."

"You," she panted hoarsely while looking him in the eyes.

His hand moved away and half of her was relieved while the other part felt empty and ached for more. "Are you satisfied? It was you."

"No. I won't be satisfied until *I am* inside you. Not my fingers. I won't be satisfied until I hear you scream my name in your release and your long legs are wrapped around me. Until then, I'll be satisfied that every time you hear a drum, you'll imagine my fingers rubbing against you."

Just his words made her body shudder. Dakota aimed one last furious glare his way before getting to her feet to join the audience in their roaring applause.

Chapter 12

Dakota stared at the driver as he opened the door to the car and let her out. A few steps and she would be in the hotel, a few more steps and she would be alone in an elevator with Blake. As she stepped out of the car and Blake took his place beside her, she looked at a small family arriving, the bellhop, the valet, everything but the man at her side. Yet she felt the heat of his gaze. She didn't want him to see that her feelings for him were growing and that she was caught up in something she not only didn't understand but couldn't control.

Something live and intense ran between them, a current so strong she couldn't swim away. Tonight, as she'd closed her eyes and pleasure spiraled though her body, it had been Blake's image in her mind and his fingers on her body.

Even in the silence she could still hear his powerful voice. The sound was a rich, honeyed, controlled baritone that mesmerized her. She found that listening to Blake speak was almost as seductive as his touch. He took her hand and led her into the hotel. Although she hadn't touched a drop of alcohol, her body felt warm and relaxed. Tingly and giddy as if she'd drunk an entire bottle of wine.

"Are you all right?" he asked quietly as they waited for an elevator. The door slid open, and he stepped inside and gently pulled her toward him. Using the entrance of other people and his security team to his advantage, he pulled Dakota closer. His eyes never left her face, and even in the soft elevator lighting, he could see she looked flushed, her lips and eyes were swollen. As he looked down into eyes that were still dilated from his bringing her release with his fingers, he realized the fire he started would consume them both if not controlled.

In the midst of passion, Dakota hadn't held back, giving him a rush of desire that made him want to rip away the lace of her panties and take her against the wall outside of the concert hall; something primal called to him when she was close. And that part continued to push against his self-control. When they'd left their seats during intermission, all he wanted to do was grab Dakota and take her away to someplace private. It had taken everything he'd possessed to ignore the urge to claim her in every way.

No, he would not take her outside against a wall like a man possessed, but in a bed, where he could explore every inch of her body without interruption. Her scent hadn't gotten any weaker since he'd brought her to climax with his fingers. In fact, it had gotten much stronger. He really enjoyed the way Dakota smelled normally, but adding her arousal to the mix made her that much harder to resist.

"Dakota," he whispered.

Dakota's head came up, and she met his gaze for the first time since the end of the drumming concert. Blake's dark eyes were now deep and hooded. Her tongue darted out to wet her dry lips. "I'm fine."

"Liar," he growled.

Everything went still. Even the breath in her body as her nerves snapped tight and her skin seemed to tingle all over with passion so strong she'd never felt and didn't think she'd ever feel the same again. He was only touching her with one hand. The same hand that had brought her to climax. A shudder caught her off guard, and she closed her eyes against the erotic chill.

The elevator stopped, but it wasn't their floor. Dakota used the moment to move away from Blake, just a few inches. The space helped her regain a shred of self-control. If it were up to her body, she'd be mindlessly pressed against him like an animal in heat. Just the thought hit her like ice-cold water. What the hell was she doing?

"Dakota?"

"What?" she snapped, then realized Blake had left the elevator and was motioning for her to follow. Embarrassed, she stepped off and strode down the hall. Once she reached her room door, much to Dakota's chagrin, her fingers trembled as she dug into her purse for the keycard to her room. To make matters worse, she could smell Blake, smell him on her clothing, and sense his approach.

He stood just an inch form her side, effectively blocking the views of their watchers. He reached out and ran the back of his hand against the heat of her cheek. "Something wrong, Dakota?" he asked huskily.

Dakota gripped her teeth in response to his nearness and the effect of his touch. Hyperaware of how little control she had over her feelings, she barely managed a tight smile. "Back off, Holland."

"Invite me in."

She stared down into her purse mindlessly as his request echoed in her head and each time they were close the compulsion to give in to passion grew stronger. "No way," she said, taking a deep breath and renewing her efforts to find her key.

"You can't control this forever, Dakota."

She stiffened, and her head flew up to glare at him. "Want to bet?" she responded with a bravado she didn't feel.

His eyes darkened. "Yes, I do. We are going to make love, Dakota Montgomery. I am going to explore every inch of your beautiful skin, and I am going to be with you and inside you in every way. I won't stop with my fingers. I will sip your sweetness, drink your moans and feast on your body."

Dakota's breath caught in response to the visual images of his words. She saw them; she saw him. Naked. His muscular legs intertwined with her, his mouth sucking her breast, his hands caressing her body...

Her fingers finally landed on the square hotel keycard, and she gripped it hard. "Stop it," she whispered.

His fingertips touched her chin and forced her to look into his eyes. "I'm just started, sweetness. And one way or another, I am going to get you out of my system and when you are in my arms, and when I make love to you, there will be no holding back."

98

Without a word, she unlocked the door, opened it and closed it behind her.

Less than an hour later, Dakota had just hung up her dress when she heard a knock at her door. "Just a moment," she said, grabbing a robe. Opening the door, she expected to see a room service attendant. Instead, she blinked at Blake suspiciously.

"I love a woman who likes midnight snacks," he said, pushing the cart past her and into the hotel suite.

Dakota tightened the belt on her robe and closed the door. "As you can see, I wasn't expecting company."

Blake took a step forward, sandwiching Dakota between him and the door. He reached out and let his finger toy with the silken tendril of her hair. "Funny, I wasn't expecting your performance tonight either," he replied huskily.

Blood rushed to Dakota's cheeks as a combination of Blake's deep voice and the pull of his cologne sent a ripple of awareness through her. An image flashed though her mind; the memory of her erotic fantasy where they'd made passionate love to the beat of the taiko drums. Then just as quickly, she remembered opening her eyes and feeling his fingers touching her bare thigh. For the second time that day, her body quivered and wetness began to pool between her legs. Calling on every ounce of willpower, she managed to keep her cool. "I was caught up in the moment. But you still didn't have the right to take certain liberties."

Blake's lips curled into a possessive grin that curled her toes. "I believe I have every right. You see I can't sleep tonight." He pushed himself away from the doorjamb and wheeled the cart inside the hotel suite.

Dakota sighed wearily, then briefly glanced out into the hallway. Sure enough, two diplomatic security agents stood near the elevator banks doing a terrible job of pretending not to be interested in their conversation.

When he turned around to face her, she knew he had no intentions of leaving. She tried to use her anger at his unexpected intrusion to stave off her body's reaction, but all it took was one look at what he was wearing to blow away her mental resolve—a black turtleneck lambs wool sweater.

"Please make yourself at home," she said sarcastically.

She watched as he uncovered one of the two dishes, displaying a nicely warmed double chocolate brownie. The smile on his face broadened as her frown deepened. The last thing she wanted was for Blake to discover another one of her weaknesses. She'd wanted, no, she'd needed something to fill the lust Blake had stirred, and if she couldn't have him, she could have room service.

"The lady has a thing for chocolate."

Dakota walked over and stood on the other side of the serving tray facing Blake and pulled off the top of the second dish. "I also like vanilla ice cream."

"I noticed you've got two plates and sets of utensils here. Was I going to be invited?"

She shrugged. "No, this was going to be a private desert."

"Not a very sharing person are you?"

"I was an only child."

"I thought you grew up with O'Connor."

"After his mother died, Peter spent his summers at our ranch. My mother died while I was in high school, so before Peter it was just me."

"It shows."

Ignoring the twinkle in Blake's eyes, Dakota set the small table, poured herself a cup of hot milk from the carafe, and then sat down. "There's nothing wrong when a woman likes to get her way." Just to underscore her point, she used her fork and took a large bit out of the brownie and stuffed it into her mouth.

Blake in turn mimicked her action and managed to get some ice cream as well. "They say women use chocolate as a substitute for sex."

Aware Blake was baiting her, Dakota played along by licking the chocolate sauce from her lips. She met his eyes over the rim of her glass of milk. "Really? I've always heard that sex is a substitute for chocolate."

"And you're drinking hot milk?" he asked.

He looked at her as if painting her with his eyes. Her skin tingled as if there was a physical brush trailing over the tips of her breasts, the swell of her stomach, and sensitive inner thighs. Her tongue darted out over her lips. "I find that steamed milk helps me sleep."

"Yet, you're eating a chocolate brownie and ice cream?

Studying his confused expression, Dakota said, "I was hungry, and I liked the picture on the menu. Don't you ever get tempted to indulge in sweets?"

He shrugged a broad shoulder. "I didn't eat too many sweets when I was growing up. When I did, I liked to give them to Caroline. The expression on her face as she slowly ate each chocolate like it was a Christmas gift was all I needed."

She met Blake's stare with one of her own, enthralled with the tenderness of his expression. It was the first time since she'd met him he appeared truly affectionate, with all his emotions on the surface. "You must have a fondness for something?" she questioned softly.

Blake hesitated, measuring her for a moment; *she* was becoming his addiction. He wanted to see her, touch her, savor her mouth. There was something about Dakota Montgomery that reached out and called out to him that she was to become a part of him and a part of his life.

"Only you," he replied in a deep, soothing, hypnotic whisper.

Dakota felt her pulse race, and it throbbed noticeably in her throat. A flicker of apprehension coursed through her before she managed a relaxed smile. "You're kidding, aren't you?"

"No, I'm not," Blake answered. "When you look at me with that soft smile, something inside of me…" He paused, unable to come up with an apt description of his emotions. "Your lips are very erotic," he said instead.

She arched an eyebrow. "Erotic?"

Bound by Moonlight

He cocked his head at an angle, studying her intently. "Mesmerizing. It reminds me of looking up at the mountains when I was a boy."

Dakota laughed, the light, intoxicating sound floating up from her chest. "What a strange metaphor."

"A very fitting metaphor," he countered. "No matter the day or the time, I knew if I looked east, I would see the mountain crest, but depending on the weather or the time, it would be different yet beautiful. When you smile or when you frown it transforms your entire face and keeps me wanting to see more."

She sobered, staring at Blake and becoming increasingly aroused. His seduction was subtle, almost invisible and she found herself moving closer to him.

What hidden, invisible power did he possess that made her want to take off her robe and sleep with him? The last man she'd been with had been a generous lover, but even he hadn't affected her the way Blake Holland did.

Placing an elbow on the table, he leaned forward, a slight smile touching mouth.

Don't do this to yourself again, Dakota, she warned. *Don't let yourself fall for a man like Blake. For him this is just fun and sex and nothing more. He'll take your love and trust and give nothing in return. Remember Peter? He unintentionally broke your heart. Don't make the same mistake twice.*

She couldn't make herself believe the words completely. Blake was perhaps the most arrogant man she'd ever met, but he was going to admit the whole truth, the fact that he was one of the most desirable males she'd ever met didn't hurt.

Tonight as the vibrations of the drums flowed through her body, she'd forgotten about the person or persons forcing Peter to betray his country and her own annoyance at the assignment. She should have been doing so many things. It wasn't just that her job as a journalist pushed her. She pushed herself to do more, to write more. Yet since she'd arrived in Japan, Dakota had barely written more than a few emails. She didn't know what it was about Blake Holland, but something about him made everything else besides being with him seem irrelevant.

"Now that expression is nearly as mysterious as it is seductive," Blake said with a smile.

"Just trying to figure you out," she replied.

He stood and walked over to her. "Any progress?"

She shook her head. "No. I need more details. Unlike the government, I don't have access to inter-agency information and detailed background records. I barely managed to get two pages of personal information on you, Blake Holland."

"Ask me."

"Ask me?" she repeated as he took her hands and led her over to the sofa.

"Ask me what you want to know." They both settled on the coach and Dakota noticed that Blake hadn't let her hands go. A thousand and one questions crowded her mind, but the second she raised her head to ask, all of them disappeared. His eyes were dark as sin. His closely shorn head with its symmetrical smooth roundness invited her fingers, while his strong jaw and firm lips begged for kisses.

Dakota scolded herself for her lack of focus. It seemed that close proximity to Blake Holland led to a temporary loss of common sense, and she needed every advantage she could muster.

"Are you all work and no play? And if not, what do you play?" she asked, totally confused at where the thought had come from.

Blake's brow furrowed, obviously taken off guard by the question as she was. Several heartbeats passed, and Dakota watched as his expression took on a thoughtful stare. "Funny you should ask that question. It's been years since I played a round of golf for pleasure instead of business."

Dakota leaned over, rested her head on his shoulder and smiled. There had to be some kind of cosmic trick being played on the both of them. Some renegade angel attempting to pay her back for some unknown grievance. Because that would be the only way to explain how perfectly they fit together. She'd known Blake for less than a week, but her body *knew* his as if it were a missing piece.

"I wouldn't have pictured you as a golf man."

"And what kind of man would you have pegged me for?" Blake asked as he put his arm around her shoulders and played with her hair.

She playfully squeezed his arm muscles. "Maybe boxing or martial arts. These strong arms of yours aren't gym made."

"You're right. When I'm in the States I like to spend as much time as I can working on the house."

It was Dakota's time to raise an eyebrow. "House?"

"After getting transferred back to Washington, D.C., I happened to be driving around in Prince George Country and came across this abandoned Colonial brick house. I actually bought the house for the land and trees. I spent a small fortune renovating the inside, but there's still plenty to do."

"So you're a Jack-Of-All Trades type, huh? High-powered executive, trade negotiator, and Mr. Fix-It? You are going to make some woman extremely happy one day."

"I would settle for making you happy tonight, Dakota."

Unsure of how to respond, she nibbled the inside of her lips and stared straight ahead. "As much as I would like to believe you Blake, I don't know enough about you to trust your sincerity."

His fingers began to massage the back of her neck, and Dakota relaxed even more. "We'll have to work on the distrustful nature of yours."

"I'm a journalist. Our main creed is to always check the facts and validate them."

"You do realize this conversation is off-the-record," Blake warned, his tone both teasing and serious.

For the first time since she'd chosen her career path, Dakota regretted the instant suspicion that came with the title. Her aim as a journalist was never to intrude upon people's daily lives, but the events she investigated were always man-made, and to get to the heart of the truth, she needed to see into the heart of the man. Yet, the line between business and personal for her should never have been crossed. But the moment she had responded to his kiss, their relationship became very personal.

Blake slowly tilted her head upward and touched his mouth to hers once, then twice. His eyes locked with hers.

"I don't think you want this to be in print," he whispered, leaning closer to her lips. "Unless you want the world to know how your kisses taste like milk chocolate."

"And your mouth tastes like vanilla, your eyes remind me of sweet butterscotch when you're aroused," she managed to respond. She pulled away and placed a finger to his lips to convey the seriousness of what she was about to say. "What happens between us, Blake, stays between us. From the first moment we met in the gym, I knew that I couldn't write about you because I couldn't be objective."

He didn't respond to her statement verbally, but physically, she followed the direction of his eyes to watch as his fingertips traced down the edge of her robe and stopped at the belt. Her heartbeat seemed to pulse in anticipation as his hand paused. Sensing he was waiting for some indication on her part, Dakota placed her hand on his, urging him to continue.

"Blake?" Dakota breathed, recognizing the look in his eye, understanding it. The deep look of desire in his eyes made a heated shudder pass over her skin, and when he released a deep breath, she undid the rope and shrugged off her robe to stand before him clad in her undergarments.

Blake had done some difficult things in his lifetime, but at the moment nothing compared to how hard it was not to rip off the black silk slip and take Dakota straight to bed. He swallowed and curled his hands into fists so she would not see how his fingers trembled.

His finger reached out and caressed her cheek as his eyes devoured her. "You're going to be my downfall, Dakota," he murmured. She was too beautiful, too gentle, too perceptive. And somehow in the short time he'd known Dakota, she'd managed to claim a part of his heart he'd thought was dead. Blake buried those thoughts deep, at least for the moment, under something even more now and infinitely stronger...the wave of inarticulate desire that swept over him.

He slid the straps off her shoulders, and the slip fell, pooling at the bottom of her feet. She stepped out and he backed up. For a minute, Blake let his eyes feast on the sight of her body, naked but for a black bra and matching panties. Just as he'd both feared he'd never see her that way, sometimes he'd feared he would. He knew with utter certainty Dakota would be like no other woman in his life. That she would forever be in his mind and he would never be able to erase her from his memories. And knowing that, certain of it, he couldn't stop himself.

Blake walked around and unhooked her bra strap, then when he faced her again, he drew a line from her neck to the valley of her breasts while watching her eyelids flutter. He pushed her bra down, baring her breasts to his gaze. Any thought of future regrets vanished.

Her breasts were high, round, the nipples pebbles to hardness.

A ragged sigh escaped him. "Do you know what you do to me?"

Dakota's head was tilted back, her eyes half-lidded as she looked up at him with beautiful eyes, and he could see her losing it a little. "No...Tell me," she said softly.

"May I show you instead?" He moved his hand and gently cupped her breast, pulling his head away from her long enough to look up and catch her gaze...then he slowly guided the cocoa-tinted nipple into his mouth. Dakota hissed in her breath lightly. Blake's other hand cupped her behind, squeezing the round flesh...then he pulled her closer, so close she had to put one hand on his shoulder to steady herself against his chest. He sucked her nipple gently, his eyes still holding hers, then he gripped it lightly between his teeth, teasing the tip with a series of butterfly-light flutters of his tongue.

Before he knew what he was doing, he was sinking his hands in her hair, entangling his fingers in the thick, heavy, length and kissing her hard, bruising her with his mouth. He felt a shock go through his body as their lips touched, slicing through his heart and stomach and into his sex, which was hard and throbbing with an unvoiced want, pressing against the tight line of his pants, and he needed her, wanted her. And even though her profession put them on opposite sides, for one brief moment in time it didn't matter to Blake…none of it mattered.

Her finger ran up and down his pants. "Take them off," she whispered against his mouth.

Blake could barely breathe at her whispered command. He didn't think it would have been possible to want her more, but somehow she'd managed to make that happen.

"Bossy little thing, aren't you?" he growled. Blake took the delicate nub of her ear between his teeth and nibbled. A shudder ripped through her body, and he used her distraction to pick her up and carry her into the bedroom. He positioned Dakota next to the bed and held her there.

Looking down into her heavy lidded gaze, as their eyes locked his heart stopped. Dakota was with him…no, not Dakota…this was not Dakota, the journalist whose cool confidence could charm a room of diplomats and exposés topple corporations. No, this was the mate he'd dreamed about who clung to him. Her fingers slipped underneath his shirt and scratched a hard, wicked line over the skin of his shoulders and chest.

He sucked in a sharp breath as her sharp little teeth nibbled his lips, sucking hungrily at his tongue as he felt his fingers slip down her back, over her hips and thighs, and then he had her in his hands and he was lifting her, laying her on the bed, and moving between her long, luscious legs.

Once he laid her down naked on the bed, their movements were frenzied, the fumbling, breathless gestures of lovers too long apart…he felt his fingers on the silk of her panties, jerking them down so hard he nearly ripped them off.

He stood up and swiftly removed his clothes, and then he came back closer and ground his raging erection against the hot place between her legs, those same limbs wrapping themselves around his waist and holding him there, tightly, as she flung back her head and moaned.

He kissed her again, harder as she reached down with her cool, electrified fingers and took his sex into her hand, squeezing it oh-so-gently and roughly at the same time. She guided him between her legs, and he forced himself to slow down. One hand grasped hers as he buried his face in her neck, smelling her sweet scent, his tongue leaving hot trails up her neck's graceful line as he managed to whisper in her ear, his voice coming out like a strangled growl.

"God I want you, Dakota." His whispered confession filled the room.

Shifting his body to where she lay under him, Blake ran his fingers possessively up and down her body. He wished he could take a picture of her as she was at that moment. The darkness of her eyes, the unblemished roundness of her breasts, the dip of her stomach, the wide tangled of her hair across the white pillows.

"Then take me, Blake."

If he could, Blake would have plunged into her and given them both the relief their bodies demanded. But he pulled back and instead moved his hand over her body. He felt her skin jump as he lightly skimmed his fingertips over her breasts, across her stomach, and against the inside of her thighs before he inserted one finger into her soft heat. The wet tightness made his hips surge forward in her hand. He slowly moved his finger in and out, then added another, as he watched her pleasure. His throat crowded with emotion as a sudden tremble passed though his body. He could tell it had been a long time for them both.

Close to losing control, he whispered a quick curse. "Are you protected, Dakota?"

"No," she moaned and raised her hips in such a way that had he been positioned slightly lower, he would have been inside her. He held onto her hips and kept her from moving.

"Bad girl. Do you have condoms?"

"Nightstand," she panted.

Blake reached over, opened the nightstand to reveal foil lined packets of various sizes. As he unwrapped one, Dakota levered herself up on her elbow and delicately licked a pearly drop of liquid from his manhood. His hips instinctively jerked forward, and his hand hit against the headboard in an effort to keep his balance. "Woman, don't do that. I'm on the edge."

Her brown eyes seemed to glow hot like a cat's. She took the condom from his fingers. It took every ounce of self-control he possessed to remain still while she unrolled the latex over his length.

Task accomplished, she explored him, cupped him with her soft, slender fingers.

When he'd had all he could take, he leaned down and kissed her. He forced open her mouth and crushed her lips. Her arms wrapped around him, she could feel his penis rubbing against the inside of her leg, getting her hotter and hotter on the inside.

"I want you inside me," she mumbles into his ear. "Now."

"Your wish," he started and used his free hand to spread her legs. "Is my command."

Blake pulled her hips toward him, startling a cry from Dakota's lips as he slid inside her with a single graceful thrust. He kept his hands on her hips as he thrust into her, harder and harder, relishing the way her breasts moved with his thrusts.

"Oh Lord…" Dakota let her forehead fall against his shoulder, her eyes still closed as her chest rose and fell in hard little breaths. Blake's lips were close to her ear, his breathing harsh and raspy…and she moaned again as he ground his hips against hers, the feel of his erection delicious inside her. She moved her hands over her head and clutched at the sheets, her head thrown back, her full, sensuous lips open as she panted and fought to keep the wanton screams at bay. Blake's hands were on her hips, pulling her against him, and then he lifted her legs and hooked them over his shoulders, bring him deeper, making his thrusts sharper as he turned his head and nipping at the smooth flesh of her neck with a deep growl.

Time after time, the warm pressure built first in her back then worked its way down then out in another wave of release. Dakota's climax came so suddenly she didn't have time to get ready for it. It slammed into her with all the subtlety of a comet. She screamed, but it was breathless as her orgasm rocketed through her. She thought he cried out too, and even as the exploding pleasure thundered through her body, she prepared herself for when he would stop, when he would withdraw and she would be left with that softly throbbing but somehow empty feeling she had when it was all over...but Blake did not stop.

He let go of her legs, allowing them to slip down his shoulders. He reached down, gathering her into his arms and pulling her up close against his chest. She wrapped her legs around his waist once more and he pulled back a little, only to thrust into her again.

"Stay with me, Dakota," he whispered, his breath soft in her ear as he kissed her. The kiss was raw and primitive. His tongue entered deep into her mouth, his hands cradled her face.

Blake slowed down. As he began to move against her again, this time it was sweet, and he held her close and made love to her with slow, even, tender strokes. He caught her face in his hands, his eyes tightly closed as he kissed her. Her second orgasm came with his first. Feeling the powerful shudder of his body as they clung to each other, unexpected bliss rolled over her in heady waves.

"Oh, God..." He buried his face in her neck, groaning, the taut muscles of his shoulders and back trembling beneath her hands.

Dakota's eyes filled with tears of joy as he lowered them both back on the bed, still joined with one another. Waves of contentment washed over her skin as she drifted to sleep with the sound of his heartbeat.

Chapter 13

W hen the sound of the alarm clock finally registered in her ears, Dakota smiled as she woke up feeling better than she had in months. Without opening her eyes, she reached out to hit the snooze button, and her hand encountered flesh. Smooth, hard skin. She inhaled deeply and the air was perfumed with a lingering aroma of sex. Opening her eyes, she turned her head as memories of the night before flooded her sluggish mind.

Her stomach fluttered at the sight of Blake lying naked in the bed. Overly aware of the delicious ache between her thighs and sensitive breasts, she studied his face. She'd seen her share of handsome men from around the world, but the sight of his relaxed face as he slept would never be eclipsed in her mind. She tried to put a name to the emotion thrumming through her soul and the only match scared her stupid.

Love.

Last night he treated her body like a temple. Every touch, delicate kiss and warm breath, a beautifully read scripture of a loving prayer. As he whispered, questions of soft or hard, fast or slow, she'd given herself completely.

Dakota flashed back to what her mother had said about love—words she'd foolishly considered untrue. But the sentimental romantic part of her she'd hidden away began to believe. Love was like Momma's chocolate chip cookies; hot out of the oven with a sweet heavy scent. It was something warm and perfect. A feeling you got to have all the time. She wondered how she would get through this, having let her foolish self fall in love again.

Shaking her head, she slowly moved to get out of bed. Although sometime in the future they would have to discuss last night, she wanted to put off the conversation for as long as possible. Just as she put her feet on the floor, a hand on her arm killed the hope she could get to the bathroom without waking Blake.

"Going somewhere?" His sleep roughened voice made her shiver.

When she rotated her head around to watch him, wary brown eyes met fierce obsidian. "To the bathroom."

"We need to talk, Dakota."

"No, we need to go shower and get to the embassy. Michaels will be expecting an update." She tried to pull away, but his fingers tightened on her arm and she stilled.

Blake sat up in the bed, and she looked everywhere but his naked chest. She blushed, knowing if she looked close, there would be matching pairs of bite marks.

"Not before we talk about last night."

She gritted her teeth, counted to ten and then spoke. "You are hurting my arm."

He instantly let go, and Dakota allowed herself to take a deep breath and get her pulse under control. "Let's not make this into more than it is, Blake."

"And what is this exactly, Dakota?"

She shrugged a shoulder with a lightness she didn't feel. There was no mistaking the look of desire in Blake's gaze when he looked at her. "Sex. Two consenting adults enjoying one another for the night."

"Sex is for textbooks and television. We made love last night, and if you weren't so fixated on keeping your objectivity, you'd realize that."

"Does it matter? Last night shouldn't have happened."

"It did happen." He paused and held up three fingers. "Three times."

Dakota flushed with the memories as she stared into his eyes. "That wasn't very gentleman like."

"I have never been a gentleman, Dakota. And when we're alone, I won't be."

"Maybe we shouldn't be alone again," she stated firmly.

"Do you regret what happened last night?"

She wanted to say yes. To say she had a thousand regrets. To say making love with Blake had been the biggest mistake in her life, and if she could do it all over again, she wouldn't have kissed him back. But the truth was she'd been a willing participant in her own seduction.

"No." Her voice was a mere whisper, but it seemed to fill the bedroom. "I wanted you more than anything I've wanted before in my life. But that doesn't make this right."

Between one blink and the next, Blake had moved to sit beside her on the bed. The hand that had once held her arm, reached out and caressed the nape of her neck. Instinctively, her head fell forward. A deeply drawn breath brought his scent to her attention. And Dakota knew that for the rest of her life whenever she encountered the spicy scent of his cologne, Blake's image would come to her.

"There is no right or wrong when it comes to these matters." He spoke so close to her ear, tingles went up and down her spine.

"My primary purpose for being in Tokyo is to help Peter. And last night wasn't a part of the plan."

"I'm a master at planning, sweetheart. But life happens. And when something like this comes along, we'd be fools to let it go."

"Or bigger fools to let it happen again," she countered.

"You don't believe that."

"Don't tell me what I believe," Dakota snapped. It was too much, too soon and way too overwhelming.

She turned her back, stood and began to walk to the adjoining bathroom.

"Dakota."

She stopped halfway between the bed and the bathroom door. Her skin prickled as goose bumps prickled her flesh either from the cool room air or the intensity of his stare on her naked back. She tensed but didn't turn at the sound of him leaving the bed and walking to her side.

"Know this, Dakota. This is the only the beginning. We will make love again, very soon." And then he pulled her into his arms, plastering her naked body while he took her mouth in demanding possessive strokes. His hands cupped her bottom and his arousal jutted against her stomach. Moments later when he released her, he whispered roughly,

Bound by Moonlight

"Last night proved that you're mine. And I will not allow anyone or anything, including you, to change that."

An instant denial sprung to her lips, but she thought about what they'd shared only hours ago, what her body was feeling now, and relented as the truth sunk like a stone in her stomach.

"I'll order extra for breakfast," he said. "My suite in thirty minutes."

If ever there were a reason not to mix business and pleasure, the sight of Dakota's legs was a big one. After a quick breakfast, they'd ridden to the embassy together. The thirty-minute trip had taken place in absolute silence. Not that he minded. Just being near Dakota felt right. Soothing. For the first time in his life, the restless urge he'd fed with corporate takeovers, mergers and business deals didn't gnaw at him.

Now as he sat at his desk, automatically reading through documents and adding his signature, his mind half concentrated on his next move. Dakota Montgomery was unlike any woman he'd ever known. Last night in bed she'd been incredibly passionate. Taking just as much as he'd given, and then returning more. That morning, her coldness had first puzzled, and then angered him. Blake sat back in his chair and looked out toward the window. If he'd closed the blinds, no one would have ever known he was in Japan. And if he'd never knocked on Dakota's door last night, he would have never known how sweet she tasted, how tight and warm, wanton and innocent she could be.

The intercom buzzed, pulling Blake from his thoughts. He sat up and pressed the speak button. "Ms. Montgomery and Agent Henderson are here for your ten o'clock conference call with Director Michaels."

Not by choice, Blake kept his eyes on the computer as Dakota and Jack entered into his office. He didn't look up because he didn't know if he'd be able to keep his poker face when looking at Dakota. Instead, he took a deep breath and instantly regretted it as the jasmine scent of her perfume filled his lungs. In a room of hundred women with his eyes closed, he would be able to find Dakota by scent alone. Before last night he'd merely enjoyed her feminine aroma. Now his body craved it.

After a brief pause, he stood, waved a hand toward the small conference table near the window, and walked over toward them. Almost absent-mindedly he pulled out Dakota's chair before taking the seat next to her and focusing on the security agent first. "Afternoon, Jack." He glanced to his side. "Dakota."

Jack took a seat and handed one binder to Blake and the other to Dakota. The tall, broad shouldered man with brown hair and piercing green eyes wore the standard black suit worn by all the diplomatic security agents.

"Judging from the source of some inquiries on Dakota, Nobu's taken a very keen interest in her background and relationship with the senator. This file contains all the information and leads we've been able to gather so far using local resources. I expect that Michaels will brief us on any updates on his side of the water. As for now, the information I have is sketchy at best. The rumor mill is that Nobu has a lot riding on making sure that the United States gets limited access for finished construction material imports. We've tried to dig deeper, but that would involve direct communication with the Japanese authorities. And since that would tip Nobu off to our operation, we've torpedoed that option."

"So we still don't have a clear picture of what or how Nobu plans to derail the conference?" Dakota asked.

"That is correct."

"We're no better today than we were yesterday." Frustration leaked into her voice. "I think we need to change our approach."

"You have a recommendation?" Blake asked. He turned toward her and immediately wished he hadn't. The sight of her mocha-tinted lips threw him off kilter.

"Nobu approached me at the ambassador's party. He's obviously aware I have access to key members of the U.S. trade delegation and could be in position to deliver the strategy. Why don't we use that as leverage and change his focus to me? That would eliminate Peter as a possible security threat."

"We have to look at the bigger picture, Ms. Montgomery," Jack said.

"Dakota, please. I always think of my mother when I'm addressed by my last name."

He nodded. "Dakota, this thing is a lot bigger than just diplomatic security. Because this involves a U.S. senator and the man who could potentially become our next vice-president, it's vital we know where his loyalties lie."

"And if you discover he's co-operating with Nobu?" she asked.

This time Blake answered. He wanted Dakota to know in no uncertain terms where he stood on this. His tone was even and his face expressionless as he turned to address her question. "If we have irrefutable proof that Senator O'Connor willingly conspired to share trade secrets with Nobu Toshinori, he will be prosecuted to the fullest extent of the law."

Silence filled the office, and Blake met Dakota's pointed stare and clenched jaw. While maintaining eye contact, he reached out and dialed a number on the speakerphone. What did she want him to do? Allow a traitor to go free just because she knew him? No matter, he would stick to the plan and not allow Dakota to distract him. A knot began to form in his gut. The sooner this is over the better.

"Ms. Montgomery, may I repeat that there is an embassy car at your disposal."

Standing with over a hundred other commuters on the subway platform at the station nearest to the hotel, Dakota tried hard to disguise her nervousness. Although she'd managed to convince Blake she hadn't been feeling well and would go to the embassy later, she'd still hadn't managed to leave her hotel suite without a diplomatic security agent five steps behind her.

Dakota turned toward the voice. Phillip Davidson stood next to her. "I've never ridden on the Tokyo subway," she lied. In truth, she'd been to

Angela Weaver

Tokyo twice before, and she'd taken the train with her Japanese counter-
parts. This time would be different. If things worked according to her
plans, she would be taking the train alone.

"Right now isn't the best time. It's still rush hour."

Rush hour. She'd heard stories of the Tokyo rush hours, seen pictures
of the gloved platform attendants that shoved people in to already over-
crowded trains. At seven o'clock, Tokyo's infamous morning rush hour
was at its peak with eleven million commuters pouring into one of the
world's largest cities via a vast network of elevated trains and subway. By
nine o'clock the volume had slowed but was still somewhat heavy, which
is what Dakota was counting on. She and Phillip stood in a small ocean
of people. The train queues were down the narrow low ceiling platform
and heavily populated.

"It's an adventure." She smiled, knowing that it was a nightmare.
Phillip's expression of grim resignation made her feel a little guilty. She
liked him. She liked his relaxed demeanor and obvious dedication to his
work. That morning after Blake had left for the embassy, he'd knocked
on her door and inquired about her health, and she realized he was
genuinely concerned. Why, she didn't understand. They had barely
spoken more than a few sentences to one another since she'd been
drafted into Blake and Michaels's little plot.

"Just to let you know, ma'am, you might want to watch yourself. I've
heard stories from some of the female embassy staffers that they've had
men touching them inappropriately while riding in a crowded subway
car."

"Thank you for the warning," she replied softly. Gripping her purse,
Dakota took a deep breath and got ready as she watched the silver and
purple train pull in. The doors opened, and mentally Dakota started
counting as the doors of the train slid open and a few people got off.
She'd spent time the night before memorizing the train schedules and
knew the doors would close quickly after opening. And so Dakota
pretended to hesitate as the seconds counted down and people passed
her to enter into the train.

"Ms. Montgomery?"

Bound by Moonlight

Dakota kept her eyes on the door. Twenty seconds. Still she waited and people moved in and out of the train. Fifteen seconds. The departure bell melodies played in the station and just as the doors began to slide closed, Dakota rushed forward, turned sideways, and barely made it as the doors locked with her securely packed inside.

"Ms. Montgomery!" Phillip yelled through the train doors.

Dakota shook her head and was well aware of all the stares directed toward her. The train lurched forward, and she fell into the person at her side. After a few lurches forward then backward, she managed to gain her footing and confidence. Releasing a pent-up breath, she looked to the left for a map. Now that she'd managed to loose her watcher, the hard part really started. Now she would have to change stations and make it to her destination.

At the next stop everyone got off. The train was now only marginally crowded. Two more stops and she got off the train, no worse for the wear.

Giving a silent thank-you to the many people who'd helped her find her way through the maze of a subway, Dakota finally emerged above ground triumphant and wrinkled. Moving out of the way of pedestrian traffic, she didn't look down at street names but upward toward the sky. She'd read that the Toshinori construction company specialized in building cutting edge technology skyscrapers, and it would make absolute sense their headquarters reflect their company. Yet even after using the Internet to locate the building, she could not have anticipated seeing it in real life. Buildings, she mentally corrected as she narrowed her eyes to discover that Ikeno Tower was not one, but three towers each capped with glass pyramids.

She pulled her coat tightly around her and pushed forward.

It was only a matter of time before the diplomatic service agents caught up with her, and when they did...She shivered, not because of the cold but at that thought of Blake's reaction. No doubt about it, he would be furious. Dakota clutched her purse and tried to convince herself she was not doing anything wrong as she joined the wave of people crossing the street. Blake and the diplomatic service had gone through a lot of expense to protect their trade strategy and keep Peter's involvement with the Japanese under wraps.

But Dakota refused to follow Blake's orders to sit back and let things play out. She had to try to find something to use against Nobu. It had taken her longer than she'd liked to formulate a plan to get away from her assigned guard, but she'd done it. It was no coincidence she'd chosen to travel to the embassy by subway during rush hour. She had picked her clothes that morning in order to blend in better with those around her, putting on a dark blue jacket and skirt; she'd carefully chosen flat shoes in an attempt to minimize her height. The coat she'd chosen on a quick shopping spree in the exclusive shopping mall next to the hotel provided excellent cover. Putting a confident smile on her face, she moved forward across the plaza filled with commuters and thorough the automatic glass doors that took her into the building.

The polished marble underneath her feet and the atrium dome like ceiling above her head filled Dakota with her first sense of unease. Taking a steadying breath, she approached the front desk and managed a polite smile at the Japanese attendant.

"Good morning, how may I help you?" the attendant asked with a perfect British accent.

"I'm here to see Nobu Toshinori," Dakota stated confidently. In keeping with the Japanese culture, she lowered her eyes and waited for a response.

"You're name please?" asked the attendant.

"Dakota Montgomery," she replied, glancing downward at the computer panel.

"Ah, we are expecting you." The attendant's smile dipped slightly, and she tapped a few buttons on the screen. When she looked upward again, Dakota's trepidation grew at the woman's telltale signs of nervousness. "Please give me one moment, and I will escort you to the fifty-sixth floor."

"Thank you," Dakota replied, following the young woman across the expansive pearl-colored marble floor. The Japanese woman led her away from the general entrance and paused at the rear of the elevator bank and waved a badge over a sensor.

As the elevator door closed behind them, she briefly glanced at the LCD panel, checking the time and the temperature. The car shot up and her stomach moved down. Clutching her purse, she made a valiant attempt to keep her face neutral.

She figured she had close to an hour before the diplomatic service agents sounded the alarm and turned her photo over to the Japanese police. If everything went well, she'd be back at the embassy before lunch.

The elevator doors slid open, and Dakota stepped out. Her shoes tapped across shiny hardwood floors and she breathed temperature-controlled air with a slight hint of incense. To her right, she could see a vast array of floor to ceiling windows with phenomenal views of the city. To her left, inside glass displays on the walls and shelves, was a showcase of construction equipment replicas.

In front of her was the entrance to a large office. "We must apologize, Mr. Toshinori's last meeting has run over later than expected. He would like for you to wait in his office."

Having forgotten all about the attendant as she stared into Nobu's office, Dakota smiled. "I think it's big enough for a family of four, and I wouldn't mind the time to enjoy the view." Noticing the outside door had a view of everything in the office, she forwent the temptation to search his desk and instead took a seat close to the window. Although her eyes were focused on the comings and goings of the above-ground train, her mind was miles away.

What if I'm wrong?

Until she'd sat in that chair, Dakota hadn't allowed herself to think of Peter being anything but innocent. Yet by her coming here, she'd allowed doubt to enter her thoughts. If Peter was guilty, then Blake...

"Ms. Montgomery, what a pleasure it was to hear you were here."

Startled, Dakota turned and stood at the sound of Nobu's voice. Flanked by at least three other men, he entered the office, and as if by magic, the doors closed behind him.

120

"Please be seated." He waved a hand toward the seat she'd just vacated and took the adjacent chair. "Can I offer you something to drink? Tea, coffee, water?"

"Thank you, but I'm fine."

"When my secretary told me you were in my office, I was very surprised. But I was later informed you came alone."

"I took the subway."

"I'm doubly surprised that Representative Holland let you out of his sight much less, allowing you to come unescorted by security agents."

Dakota bristled slightly. "I am an independent journalist covering the trade talks, not a member of the team. Blake Holland does not control my actions." She shrugged lightly. "And he doesn't know I'm here."

"I see." His eyebrow rose, and Dakota caught an almost reptilian look of calculation in his eyes. A shiver of uneasiness prickled her spine as Blake's words of warning echoed in her mind.

Nobu Toshinori is a dangerous man.

She might not have believed Blake then, but she did now. For any other assignment she would have found another way, a safer way, but with Peter's career and possibly his life on the line, she couldn't afford to have doubts. They were running out of time, and if proving Peter's innocence meant dealing with the enemy, then so be it.

"Mr. Toshinori," she started.

"Nobu," he interrupted as he crossed his legs and sat back. "This little project of mine will require you and I to spend a lot of time together. I think it would be easier if we communicated on a first-name basis."

"I hope I didn't give you the wrong impression about my being here. I came in person so I could tell you I can't take on the assignment."

His expression seemed to remain almost the same after her announcement. If Dakota hadn't been paying extra attention, she wouldn't have seen the slight tightening around his eyes. "May I ask why?"

Bound by Moonlight

"As I mentioned at the Consulate reception, I'm here on assignment with the U.S. Trade Department. It may take weeks, months, or a year before I finish. During that time, and especially while I am under contract, it could be viewed as a conflict of interest if I worked for your company."

His enigmatic expression didn't change. No matter how much she attempted to study Nobu's expression to hopefully glean the smallest bit of information, Dakota failed. He gave nothing away.

"I would not think that journalists could have conflicts of interest."

"Everyone can have a conflict of interest," she responded. "There have been many times in my career where I had to choose between personal gain and my ethical responsibilities."

Suddenly, Nobu sat forward, and his dark gaze intensified. Apparently, she'd hit upon something of interest. "And how did you choose?"

"I did my job; I reported the facts without prejudice."

"And what if you have a similar situation, but it's not that you stand to win if you look the other way? What do you do if you could lose something?"

Her brows furrowed. "I don't understand what you're asking."

"What if you were in a situation where you had to choose between doing something unethical or saving the life of someone you loved?"

Dakota's heart stopped, then sped up. She sat back and didn't have to pretend to be thinking hard about his question. A myriad of thoughts ran through her mind. Blake had first assumed Peter was working for Nobu because of money. In one of the briefs she'd poured through, it had listed that United States and Japanese subsidiaries of Toshinori construction had heavily contributed to his congressional campaign. When Blake had mentioned monetary gain as a possible reason for Peter committing espionage, Dakota had vehemently disagreed. All it took was a look at the summary page of Peter's personal financial disclosure statement. His family may have first entered the United States as destitute farmers fleeing famine in Ireland, but within two generations, they had managed to amass a small fortune. Peter's father had been the oldest son, and thus his entry into the military. His death may have deprived Peter of the chance to have a semi-normal family life, but it did not leave him without financial resources.

They'd then moved on to possible political gain, Blake seemed to favor that possibility. She, on the other hand, knew Peter better. He was passionate about his career and wanted to help the American people. If there was something else that would push Peter to the point where he would actually contemplate turning over government secrets to the Japanese, it would be to protect someone he loved.

Realizing that Nobu was patiently awaiting her answer, she rubbed her forehead and managed to summon a soft smile. "Is there any other way to answer the question? I have seen some of the most horrendous things a human can witness, but I have also glimpsed the incredible acts of sacrifices prompted by love. It would be no different from yourself."

"You would choose the person's life?"

Dakota frowned slightly at his sudden amusement. "Yes."

"Ah, then we differ. In this case, I hold with my Japanese heritage versus my Western learning."

Dakota sat back in her chair as the feeling came across that she'd passed a test of some sorts. She searched her memory and hit upon a chapter from an introductory history class where the professor had pointed out the concept of individualistic versus group orientation. It was one of the fundamental differences between European and Asian values. "You wouldn't make that same decision?"

"I would not, and that is why I am president of this company. I make my decisions not just on what is for business but what is good for my country."

She nodded as comprehension dawned. "I see."

"Do you, Dakota?" he questioned, leaning forward. "Do you fully understand that I will take whatever steps necessary to ensure my Japan's continued success, and I firmly believe there are some domestic sectors that should never be open to foreign competition."

Bound by Moonlight

"I see," Dakota replied. She stood up and faced Nobu. This time because she was wearing her flats, she didn't tower over the Japanese executive, but she was still taller.

His narrowed eyes bore into hers and he nodded. "I believe we have an understanding, don't we?"

"Yes. Now if you don't mind, I need to get back to the embassy."

"Of course, I'll have my personal car take you back."

She shook her head. "I can take the subway."

"I insist. You are a guest of my country, and I want to make sure you enjoy your stay."

Dakota nodded, seeing the futility of her protests. "Thank you."

She turned and walked toward the door as her hand reached out to turn the knob, Nobu's voice stopped her.

"And, Dakota?"

She paused without turning her head.

"Please send Peter my regards and convey I very much look forward to our meeting next week."

Her hand pressed down on the knob, and she couldn't walk out of the office fast enough.

⚜

As the clock struck nine o'clock, Blake threw down his pen and stared at the closed door. He had three reports, a conference call and a peer evaluation to complete before lunch, but he couldn't concentrate. Sitting back and closing his eyes, he swore, "Damn you, Dakota."

No matter how much he tried, he couldn't seem to get that woman out of his mind. All of his thoughts were full of her; the sight of her lying naked in the bed; her dark hair flowing over the pillow; the feel of her skin, smooth as silk; and her scent. Something sweet and soft, jasmine, combined with the scent of her body in a combination that was heady enough for him to drown in.

He felt his body harden as he remembered Dakota's kisses. The softness of her lips on his skin. The heat of her mouth as she'd kissed her way down starting at his temple and ending on his erection. As a grown man, he'd never cried, but last night he'd been close. Too close. In his mind's eye he relived the moment again.

"Let me show you the pleasure that you've shown me, Blake" Dakota whispered and lowered her head.

She planted a kiss on either side of his thigh, eliciting a harsh gasp.

Seemingly emboldened, she kissed him again, running her tongue along the inside of his groin. Every thought fled from his mind as she continued to lick the edge of his groin, then suddenly planted a kiss on the tip of his shaft. If Blake had been aroused before, and enjoying himself before, he hit new heights now.

Dakota licked slowly along his shaft, then slid her lips over the top and slowly worked her way down, using her tongue. The action sent Blake over the edge, and he was beyond murmuring now: he was beyond anything except wordless moans as Dakota worked her mouth up and down his erection.

She sucked harder, working her tongue all over the tip, and running one hand up and down his shaft. And he'd used every drop of willpower to stop his release and the resolute object that was his will met the irresistible force of Dakota's tongue—and gave way. Blake's release came with a shout, and she'd stayed with him until the end, when he'd spent himself and couldn't remember how to breathe.

He reached down and pulled her close. Blake opened his mouth to speak, but her fingers pressed against his lips, urging him to remain silent for a moment longer.

"Some women might be reluctant to do that, Blake, but I am not those women," she said with a serious look.

He kissed the fingertip on his lips and smiled. "I am not like most men, and I've known from the night I first saw you that you were not like most women, Dakota. That was extraordinary."

The steady ring of the phone pulled Blake from his daydream. He shook his head and took a deep cleansing breath and let it out slowly.

Bound by Moonlight

Shifting uncomfortably in his chair, he picked up the phone. No doubt about it. Today was going to be a long day.

Chapter 14

W e have a problem."

Peter closed his eyes and reopened them as he stared at the man sitting across from his executive desk. He hadn't slept at all last night and the truth be told, he should have remained at home for the day. But at least while he was in his office in the Russell Senate Building, Nobu's spies could not track him.

In less than two hours, he had a closed-door meeting with the committee on foreign relations. His mind should have been focused on analyzing the latest information on Iran's nuclear ambitions, but instead his chief of staff sat in front of him. Normally, the man who was instrumental in his election never lost his composure. But, Ambrose's wrinkled brow set off warning bells in his head.

"What's happened?" His outward calm was totally inconsistent with his inward nervousness. Despite his best efforts to keep his attitude and demeanor the same, the strain of the past week was beginning to take its toll.

"I'm not really sure. I need you to tell me everything that you've done in the past month, Peter."

Unease snaked through Peter. There were three people he trusted with his life. Mitchell Montgomery, Dakota, and Ambrose. None of them knew his secret. How could he tell the people who believed in him he'd fathered a son with an underage Japanese girl? How could he look them in the eyes and explain his secret might have compromised his integrity, but also put the mother of his child and his son at risk?

Bound by Moonlight

"An old Army buddy of mine at the N.S.A. tipped me off this morning. Someone high up the food chain is in the process of putting you under a microscope."

Peter shrugged and tried his best to hold his gaze level. "How is this any different from the last time they checked up on me? Someone probably wanted to even out the odds with the State Department budget reallocation hearings next month."

"It's more than that, Peter. Don't try to lie, I've seen you hunched over a toilet puking your guts out after a speech. If we're going to get through whatever this is you're involved in, I need to know everything, and I need to know it now."

He sat back, drew a deep breath, and simply said, "I have a son."

Four words. Peter would have never thought four words would have had such a profound effect on his life, but the more he thought about it, the more it made sense. Significant moments in life had few words. The day he'd come home from school to find Mitchell Montgomery sitting outside of their house in a beat up Ford pickup truck, the Sergeant had used three words. "I'm sorry son."

That was all he remembered. Not the details of his father's death or that he'd saved lives. Just the first three words.

Ambrose frowned. "Did you just say that you have a son? When the hell did that happen?"

"Fourteen years ago."

"You met her in college?"

"While I was stationed in Japan. Her family lived near the base."

"So you got a Japanese girl pregnant. What the hell? Is she the Prime Minister's daughter?"

Peter managed a dry chuckle at the thought. "No. Her parents were school teachers. Akiko was still in high school when we met. We saw each other for about three months before I was transferred to Germany."

"You didn't know she was pregnant?"

Peter shoved his hands through his hair roughly, stood up and began to pace back and forth. "I had no idea. Damn it, she didn't even cry when

I told her I had to leave. She just stood there and looked at me, Ambrose. She looked at me like a wounded animal."

A sharp pain he had managed to ignore for the past thirteen years touched his heart, reminding him of the reason he had fallen in love with her. She'd possessed such a loving, gentle and hopeful spirit. After his parent's death, he'd given up on almost everything and everyone until the early Saturday morning Akiko had accidentally hit him while she was riding her bicycle.

"What else, Peter?"

Ambrose's questions snapped him back to the present. "She was underage when I met her."

"Christ," Ambrose cursed. "We need to call an emergency meeting. I can get Douglas in from New York to help with the public relations. If we get to press before anyone else does, we've got a decent chance of keeping this from turning in to a media feeding frenzy. Now, the main thing is we try to suppress the woman's age. Maybe make her older, and we need her co-operation and the boy's."

Peter shook his head. "What Akiko feels or thinks right now is the least of my worries. Ambrose, I'm being blackmailed."

"What?"

"Nobu Toshinori has threatened to kidnap Akiko and my son."

"Slow down a minute, Peter."

Peter managed to stop pacing. "I don't have minutes, Ambrose. I've got to walk into the foreign relations committee and sit there for hours, while contemplating that my son and his mother might be picked up and held against their will to ensure my cooperation."

"What does he want?"

"Information on the upcoming trade conference. He wants the U.S. strategy ahead of time so he can give it to the Japanese negotiators."

"That's treason, Peter. You can't do it."

"I can't let them kill my son!" he halfway shouted angrily. It was an impossible situation, and they both knew it, but Peter didn't need anyone else telling him what he could or could not do. There were too many unknowns he had to deal with, including the possibility that Nobu would go after Dakota as well. All he knew for certain was he wouldn't stand by and let anyone threaten the people he loved.

Ambrose stood and faced him. "Calm down. I'm only here to help."

Like a match blowing out, Peter's anger disappeared and left him feeling hallow. "I know. I'm having a tough time keeping it together."

"Let me make some phone calls. See if I can find a C.I.A. source or two that can find the woman and your son."

"I've already hired the best. If you pull someone else in, that increases the chance Nobu will get wind that I'm not cooperating, and he could move them."

Ambrose moved closer to pat Peter on his shoulder. "You're stressed out and in no condition to make decisions of this magnitude alone."

Peter shook his head. He'd thought of nothing else since seeing the picture. If they didn't succeed in getting his son before Nobu's deadline, he would have no choice but to hand over the documents. He'd thought about handing over false documents to stall for more time, but it only increased the risk. What he needed most was leverage. Peter's chest went tight. Last night he'd called Dakota on the pretext of discussing her father. What he'd really wanted to know was how close she was to Blake Montgomery.

He hated the thought of deepening Dakota's involvement in his affairs, but he was running out of options.

"Peter?"

"You're right."

"Yeah, well that's what you pay me the big bucks for. So let me try and find out if it's Nobu or someone else trying to dig up Intel on you."

"What do I need to do?"

"Besides take a drink and a long walk? I need you to concentrate on making sure the committee chairman doesn't insult the sheik of Omar at the meeting. Think you can handle it?"

Peter managed a weak laugh. Somehow his mind felt lighter as if he'd spent half the morning sequestered in the confessional. "Yeah. I'll do my best."

"All kidding aside. We need to plan for worst case scenarios later today."

"Come by the townhouse later tonight," Peter said. "I've got a fundraiser this evening but I'll leave early."

Ambrose started toward the door and stopped. "I'll stop and pick up the coffee and doughnuts. Looks like this is going to be a long one."

❧

"Blake, its two o'clock in the morning. Why don't you call it a night? Hell, you can call it a week. We're set for the conference."

Blake looked toward the door as his senior staffer, Richard McNab, leaned in the doorway. Settling back in his leather chair, he raised his hands over his head and stretched. Muscles long used to being hunched over protested from the movement. Blake shook his head. The last place he wanted to go was his hotel room. He'd been on edge since the moment he'd picked up the phone earlier that morning. The diplomatic security agent assigned to Dakota had somehow lost her in the subway. His heart rate accelerated at the mere thought. The labyrinth of the Tokyo subway could be dangerous for foreigners, especially when Dakota could be Nobu's newest target.

He'd barely managed not to run out of the building to search for her. It was after he'd remembered he'd placed a tracking device in her purse that he'd regained a sliver of self-control. He'd hurriedly keyed in the devices unique identification number to the GPS locator, and when the map displayed, the blinking dot representing Dakota Montgomery was in the last place on earth he wanted her to be.

Toshinori Corporation

Anger coursed through his veins, and even hours after he'd discovered she'd disobeyed him, he could still wring her pretty little neck. And that reason alone was why he had yet to leave the embassy.

"Blake, you really should get out of here." Richards voice broke into his thoughts.

Bound by Moonlight

"I just want to make sure we haven't missed anything," Blake lied. "These Japanese negotiators are sharp. If we don't put it in the agreement, they'll either do a fully or heavy tariff on the items."

"If it's not in there, it will be in there by the time we get to the table. It's my job to work on the details and make you look good. If you're here half the night, then I look bad."

Blake stood and walked around his desk. "This has nothing to do with my lack of faith in your work."

"So what other reason do you have to be here this late?"

He shrugged a shoulder. "Habit."

"Break it. If it were up to me, I wouldn't see your face until the day before the conference. You're my boss, so I can't order you to get out and explore Tokyo. Remember that reporter is here not just to cover the conference, but to extol the virtues of the new U.S. Trade Representative. So why don't you give Dakota Montgomery the impression we trade representatives are a group of people who not only work hard but play hard, too."

Blake picked up his jacket and headed for the door. "I'll think about it."

Richard's mouth kicked up at one corner. "Good."

Half an hour later, Blake stepped out of the embassy car and made his way to his hotel suite. Darkness still blanketed the city. Soon the sun would nudge against the eastern sky, lighting the city and bringing it alive. After entering into his room, he turned on the lights, threw his jacket on the sofa and stared at the closed door between his and Dakota's suite.

It would have been so easy for him to shower and lay in his bed, but he knew he wouldn't sleep; couldn't sleep until he saw her again and confronted her about seeing Nobu. Although the security agents didn't suspect she really hadn't been lost like she'd claimed, he knew. That knowledge buried. What else would Dakota be willing to do for Peter?

Unable to pace any longer, Blake tested the adjoining door and found it unlocked. He walked into Dakota's bedroom with every intention of confronting her about her deception but the scent of her perfume drew him in just as much of the sight of her asleep. The planes of his face shed their hardness, and tenderness shown in his eyes.

Instead of waking her he took a seat in one of the chairs and watched Dakota sleeping, envying her for the ability to sleep so soundly that not even the occasional sounds of the city disturbed her. As the Tokyo nightlights and the half-moon spilled in through the open windows, he watched her. When was the last time he'd watched the rhythmic rise and fall of a woman's chest while she slept, listened to the soft little sound of her breathing. When was the last time his heart had damn near stopped with fear. And the answer, terrified him. The last time he'd felt such an intense fear was the night before his mother died. He'd never really known how much he could love a person until he could no longer pick up a phone and call her on the phone. He'd been just as afraid when he'd gotten the call from the DS agent. Blake leaned his head back and his heart slumped with the heaviness of his newest revelation.

He hated to wake her. Hated to disturb her. Sometime during the night the comforter had slipped down, riding along her waist. She slept on her side, with one leg stretched out, the other crooked at an angle. Her arms curved around the second pillow. With her dark hair spilling across the pillow, Dakota looked peaceful. Her long eyelashes lay still. He was tempted to lift a hand, to touch, to smooth the strands from her cheeks, to kiss her parted lips.

He really was losing it.

They weren't there for a lover's rendezvous. They were there because Michaels believed Dakota would be the key to Senator Peter O'Connor's downfall. They were there because as much as Michaels wanted Dakota's help, Blake wanted her affection. And while he knew intellectually that Dakota cared for Peter like a brother, it didn't stop him from being jealous. She'd not only disobeyed him, but could have also needlessly put herself in danger.

And as illogical as everything was, the only true thing was that he loved her.

That thought alone should have bothered him, but it didn't. He wanted more from Dakota. He wanted to know more about the lady sleeping soundly in the bed. The woman who'd come alive in his arms the other night. There were a million and one things he couldn't discover about Dakota from the confidential file he'd read earlier that day. He wanted to know her favorite color, what she'd experienced in Sierra Leone, how had she managed to keep her sanity when surrounded by famine and poverty.

He'd never been the impulsive type. Everything had to be planned, everything could be controlled. It had become second nature for him growing up, and he had never learned to let go. His little sister had once said he didn't know how to be spontaneous. But he had been. Once. In another lifetime. They'd all been. He and his mother. She'd taken him on long walks in the mountains, bus trips to the city. But all of it had ended the day his mother had discovered the man she loved had another family.

He remembered the promise he'd made to his little sister to take some time and enjoy life. His lips inched upward with the thought. He would hold off talking about her unscheduled visit for a while and gain her trust. And until then, Dakota Montgomery would see him in a different light, and he would find out more about the woman who'd become his waking and sleeping obsession.

Chapter 15

Lord this ought to be a crime, Dakota thought as the alarm sounded. Automatically, her hand reached out to hit the snooze button. She rolled over, only to hear it again ten minutes later. Last night, she'd spent hours on her laptop searching every information source and calling in every favor she had available to learn more about Nobu. She'd spoken with her father and as obliquely as she could she warned him to be aware of any strangers around the ranch. Although her body lay relaxed, her mind was already dreading the day to come.

She knew with 100 percent certainty that the D.S. agents had informed Blake of her going missing yesterday. But what she didn't know was if Blake suspected if her getting lost had been an "accident."

Turning her face closer into the pillow, she released a pent-up breath. It had been pure luck that her diplomatic escort had believed her story of being lost on the subway. Seeing Nobu in person hadn't helped as much as she'd hoped. Dakota still didn't know how to help Peter. From the beginning she figured Nobu would try and frame Peter. But having come face-to-face with him, she had the distinct impression that Peter wasn't his only source for information on the trade conference.

Yet, as much as Nobu's implicit threat frightened her, Blake's reaction to the news was a far more pressing matter. The hotel alarm clock went off for a third time. Dakota reached over to turn it off completely when the phone rang. More awake, she dragged the blankets away, sat up and took the receiver off the cradle. "Yes."

"Open the door for me."

She heard a click, and then stared at the phone blankly. It took her a moment to realize he'd hung up the phone. Dakota shook her head.

The husky bass in Blake's voice sent tremors throughout her body. All she had to do was close her eyes to remember each time he'd kissed her: the way he covered her mouth with his and his tongue mated with hers, the feel of his teeth gliding across her skin, his lips suckling her breasts.

She stood up, grabbed the robe from the foot of her bed and padded out of the bedroom, to the bathroom. Five minutes later after she'd finished half of her morning ablutions, she was at least halfway present-able. Taking a deep breath, she pushed down the door handle connecting the two hotel suites, then frowned. The door was unlocked. She opened it and stood back. The sight that greeted her eyes would warm her for weeks to come.

While inhaling the rich aromatic smell of coffee, her eyes feasted on both the table full of breakfast food and Blake. Behind him the sun had begun to rise over the thin morning fog blanketing Tokyo. Blake leaned against the doorway between the bedroom and the living area of the suite. He was smiling in such a boyish way her heart stopped, and she had to fight the urge to cross the space between them and kiss him. He was wearing jeans and a long sleeved Polo shirt that showed off the muscles of his arms along with the outline of a nice solid chest. Not knowing what to say, she asked an obvious question. "What happened to your clothes?"

"Good morning, Dakota," Blake said, crossing his arms over his chest and pinning her with an amused look.

Embarrassed at her lack of manners, she gave him a dry look. "Good morning."

"I thought we might have breakfast before heading out to the museum."

"Museum?" she repeated puzzled. "Is there an event you didn't tell me about?"

"Not that I know of, but you did fail to tell me about your subway adventures yesterday morning."

Careful not to betray the dart of fear prickling her stomach, she shrugged a shoulder and avoided making direct eye contact. "Yeah, what of it?" she responded in a defensive tone. "Everyone gets lost on the subway sometimes."

Blake stepped away from the doorway and waved her over toward the small table. "True, but you had Agent Davidson calling individual subway stations trying to locate you."

"I apologized." Dakota waited for Blake to pull out her seat, and then she sat down.

He sat across from her and poured a little cream in his coffee. She watched as he paused to inhale the steam rising from the mug before taking a sip. The movement would have been nothing special on another man, but somehow he made it sensual and sexy. Shaking off those thoughts, she prepared her own coffee and sat back on the chair trying hard to breathe deeply and calm her nerves.

Blake stared at her over the rim of the cup. "You shouldn't have left him."

Locked in his gaze, she forgot the twinge of guilt brought on by meeting with Nobu against Blake's wishes. Dakota's slender jaw clenched slightly at the hint of censure in his voice. She was a grown woman, not a child. Just because they'd made love, he didn't have claim on her. Struggling to keep her tone even, she ripped a piece of fresh bread and buttered it. "It would be a waste to ruin such a nice morning with an argument about something that happened in the past, wouldn't it?"

Blake smiled. "Yes, it would."

He was giving up way to easily, she thought. But then again, every-thing about that morning was too easy. It seemed that everything outside of the hotel suite had disappeared and they were cocooned into a private, intimate space. A powerful connection flowed between them. But as much as she wanted it, it wasn't the way things were supposed to be. When it came to Blake, her emotions warred with her commonsense.

They spent the next twenty minutes talking about the latest interna-tional news, conference details and embassy matters. Blake was certain the ambassador to Japan would be chosen to succeed the retiring secre-tary of state, but Dakota was adamant the man didn't have the necessary congressional support to pull off the coup.

Blake chuckled. "You sure about that?"

She met his gaze. "Absolutely."

"Then you won't mind taking a bet on it?"

"Okay, what are the stakes?"

"You have to grant me one wish."

"And if I win?" she asked.

With an undeniably sexy tone, he said, "Then I have to grant you one wish." This was beginning to sound like something out of a movie. Despite her better judgment, she took the bet.

The day was one of those nice pre-spring days complete with sunny skies and cool breezes. Nestled in the backseat of the embassy car, Dakota peeked at Blake out of the corner of her eyes as she watched the passing Tokyo landscape. She couldn't help but peek. The man looked good in jeans. Too good, she crossed her legs at her ankle and wished she'd taken more time to dress that morning. Although she was completely comfortable in her jeans and turtleneck, she would have looked better if she'd at least put on mascara.

Relaxing into the cool leather seat, she placed her hand on the chair rest and was pleasantly rewarded when Blake rested his hand sat atop hers. A secret smile played on her lips. She wondered what it was that attracted her to this man. She admired his sense of total control and concentration.

She felt warmth at his smile and laughter, enjoyed the way his eyes made her feel as though she were the most beautiful woman in the world, and she loved the way he moved. The way he walked into a room with confidence and assuredness, not to mention the intense eyes, the body, the hands and the man's kiss.

"It's been a while since I've been to the museum," Blake said, breaking into the comfortable silence.

"You must know I'm curious as to what's behind this sudden change of heart. Everyone at the embassy who would talk to me mentioned you're a classic workaholic."

He chuckled. "True. But I've been temporarily relieved of my duties for the next few days."

"Better translated, your team mutinied."

"Something like that." His eyes twinkled, and the sight made everything disappear except the unfurling warmth on her heart.

"So where exactly are we going, and why are we going to a museum?"

"The Edo-Tokyo Museum. The ambassador mentioned it was one of the best-kept secrets in Tokyo."

Dakota's brow rose. "I've read every article, interview and document I could find that had your name on it Blake. You like technology, sports and the outdoors. Here we are in the city that boasts more tech toys than any other place on earth, yet you're choosing to go to a museum…" She was fishing for information, and they both knew it. Nothing could make her believe she was the reason behind the sudden change in his behavior. One night in bed couldn't have done it. But a sliver of fear skipped her heartbeat because as much as she didn't want to acknowledge it, making love with Blake had changed her. When this was over and she left Japan, Dakota would be leaving a part of herself with him.

"Your information would be right. But so is mine. I have it on good authority that a certain journalist has a passion for both history and writing."

Dakota turned her body toward Blake, very aware that by the next morning word of their relationship would be flying across the embassy communications network. Within twenty-four hours, it would be general knowledge amongst the journalist circles. Within forty-eight hours her father would be ringing her mobile phone.

"Your source is correct. I grew up steeped with history. My grandfather was very proud of his Sioux heritage. He would spend hours telling and retelling stories his father told him about the clashes between the U.S. government and the tribe. Grandfather was born a few years after their tribe was forced from the reservation in the James River to Crow Creek Reservation on the east bank of the Missouri. He spoke about his own uncle who had been hung after a false accusation of rape by a white farmer's wife." Dakota swallowed back a hot rush of tears as her grandfather's voice seemed to echo in her mind.

"I apologize, I didn't mean to stir up bad memories," Blake said softly.

She shook her head in the negative and smiled. "You shouldn't apologize. For every negative story, I have a million happy ones. Would you believe my grandmother was one of the few women to go out and round up the herd? Not to mention she was a Black woman. Most of the pictures we have are of her on top of her horse. There's a strong belief that my grandfather didn't just marry her because of her looks, but that she was the only person who could outride him."

"One day soon, I want to hear all of your stories, Dakota. Not just the ones about your family, but the tales that affected you so deeply that you can't write about them."

Blake reached out and trailed a finger over her cheek. At the look of tenderness in his expression, something within her softened. It was a feeling such as she had never experienced until this moment. And as her mind examined it like a puzzle, a glimmering of understanding began to form. But just as the definition of the emotion that ran through her body began to form, Dakota pushed it away. Now was not the time for to examine her heart. Instead, she entwined her hand in his and sat back. "It will take more than a day for all that."

"I'll give you all the time you need." He grinned.

"I want to hear your stories, too, Blake."

The sparkle in his eyes cooled. For a moment, she wanted to take back her words.

"I don't have a lot of happy memories of my childhood, Dakota."

"I don't need happy all the time," she said softly.

He nodded and returned his attention toward the window as the car rolled to a stop. Dakota zipped up her jacket and buried her hands in her pockets as she stepped out. The wind whipped through her hair, and she stared ahead at the concrete structure where old Tokyo and modern Tokyo metropolis met. Blake took her hand and moved forward. The building stood up above its base like a capital T and seemed to float on air. Yet as they moved closer, she could glimpse part of the museum from the other side. The shape seemed to be familiar. "Is it just me or does it look like a futuristic Japanese castle?" she asked.

He laughed, and the sound echoed in the open courtyard. "For the moment it's just you. I'm not up on my Japanese architecture. Talk to me about art and I can participate in the conversation."

"All right. What is your favorite piece of art?" she asked.

He stepped closer and on the pretext of adjusting the collar of her coat, leaned down. "You," he murmured against her ear.

If the definition of art was the creation of beautiful things, then the woman in front of him had to be one of God's masterpieces. She appealed to every one of his senses. Dakota's breasts, which fit perfectly in his hands, the mocha brown of her nipples, the curve of her stomach, the soft bow of her mouth. He couldn't get enough of the sound of her voice as she sobbed out her pleasure when they made love. And just her scent alone could arouse him. Blake knew he would never tire of her brown eyes as she looked at him now, watched as they darkened with the memory of their lovemaking. His body grew hard and aroused.

"What are you doing to me?" Dakota asked him. "You make me crazy."

"How crazy?"

"It's close to freezing out here, but I'm not. You touch me, and I want to make love to you."

"Would it make you feel better if I said you have the same affect on me?"

"Yes."

He smiled and took her hand. "Feel better."

The sound of voices speaking in Japanese snapped Dakota back to reality. Taking her place alongside Blake, they approached the escalator of the museum and joined the tour group heading for the entrance. It seemed people had barely begun to trickle in. She was sure the place would be packed by noon.

They stood next to one another on the escalator, and Dakota relaxed into the curve of his arm. After being constantly escorted by one DS agent, it didn't faze her when she saw two of them waiting at the museum entrance. She drew in a deep breath, and the masculine smell of Blake's cologne smelled good. So good that the whiff alone brought every nerve ending in her body to life. Clearing her throat, she concentrated on his last words. "Let me guess, you've got a lifetime pass to the Louvre?"

He shook his head. "Wrong. Metropolitan Museum of Art in New York. I went every other week when I worked in the corporate headquarters. Caroline would take the train up from D.C. to spend the weekend in the city, and we would stroll through the Impressionist Wing on the second floor after Sunday brunch."

His eyes softened and he smiled wide, his teeth white against the darkness of his skin. Dakota was transfixed by the sight. She'd never seen that side of Blake, and the abrupt change in his features was riveting. He looked relaxed, as lazily content as a lion basking in the sun, and suddenly the intimacy between them stuck her forcibly.

For a moment a stab of jealousy pricked her heart until she remembered that Caroline was his sister.

"Does your sister visit often?"

"She did until she got married. Caroline actually met her husband on the train to visit me."

Dakota smiled at the thought. "That's pretty romantic."

"You mean desperate," Blake chuckled. "I found out when he called to get my permission to propose that he'd only been on the train to meet my sister."

They entered into the large, open floored exhibition hall, feeling ready to experience the culture and an insight into the lifestyle of the Japanese people. As they crossed a bridge, a woman moved away from the side.

The stranger bowed low and gave them a beaming smile. "Good morning Representative Blake and Ms. Montgomery," the guide announced. "Welcome to the Edo-Tokyo museum. My name is Mari."

Dakota looked from Mari to Blake, then leaned over and whispered, "You have your own personal tour guide?"

He took her hand and squeezed. "There are a few perks that come with the title. Beautiful women, best seats at concerts..."

Dakota wanted to scald him with a well-placed glare, but her eyes fell upon an exquisite replica of a Kabuki Theater. She turned her attention to the guide, who was beginning to talk about how Edo, a small fifteenth-century fishing village, came to be the one of the largest cities in the world.

"Are you enjoying yourself?" Blake whispered against her ear. His hand quickly caressed her behind. Her cheeks grew hot as Dakota felt a shiver of delight ripple down her spine.

"Like a kid in a candy store," she replied.

The atmosphere of the room was soft and warm. Tall ceilings and subdued lighting served to accentuate the ancient pieces on display. It would be easy to imagine that one was transported back to the days when Tokyo was a small village.

Blake made a small hand gesture to dismiss the diplomatic security agents, and then watched Dakota. As he followed Dakota and the tour guide, he began to sense how passionate she was about Japanese culture. Seeing her eyes as she viewed the replicas of houses, collection of kimonos, kabuki costumes, fabrics, calligraphy, scrolls, paintings, stoneware, pottery, lacquer ware and samurai weaponry filled him with joy.

After a moment, he lengthened his stride and joined her at the next exhibit. But he didn't study the priceless treasures, he focused on her. It wasn't as if he didn't enjoy looking at the artifacts and learning about the Japanese culture. No, he was interested but nothing seemed to be of more importance than making Dakota smile.

"It's beautiful, isn't it?" she said quietly.

"Couldn't agree with you more."

Bound by Moonlight

Dakota turned and found Blake's eyes intent upon her face instead of the kimono and quickly looked away as her pulse sped up. Dakota noted his grin and felt her legs weaken. Her heart surrendered to the man's smile. The blood rushed to her cheeks; only Blake Holland had that effect on her.

Time seemed to hold no meaning as they went from piece to piece and took their time exploring the rooms filled with artifacts. After a while, the guide took her leave. Taking a break, Dakota and Blake sat on a small stone bench and observed the people who passed by. They smiled at a group of parents and their kids, watched as mothers tried to keep their kids from touching the museum pieces, and fathers paging through the guidebooks trying to find the nearest bathroom or exit.

Dakota wanted to laugh, but the look on Blake's face gave her pause.

"What are you thinking about so hard that you're getting wrinkles on your forehead?" she asked.

Frowning, he replied with the ghost of memory shadowing his eyes, "I was remembering my first and last trip to a museum. I was fourteen years old, and somehow my mother convinced my father to send extra money to send me on a field trip to Washington, D.C. At dinner the night before my mother mentioned he might join me at the museum. I waited in the entranceway for over an hour for my father. I found out the next day he had forgotten," he said bitterly. "It was a long time ago. I shouldn't let it bother me."

She looked around the room at the ancient artifacts surrounding them. "In some cases time is irrelevant. Does one ever stop wanting a parent's love?" Dakota asked. Her parents had always been her support. Although her father was frequently away from home, she never doubted his love. Blake, however, hadn't grown up with that bond, and her empathy for him grew stronger.

Although he was hurting, his facial expression never betrayed him. But his eyes were his undoing. The windows of the soul can never lie, and Blake's were filled with weary resignation. Uncaring of the presence of strangers, she reached over and gave Blake a hug, softly placing a kiss upon his neck. Unable to do anything else but apologize for her part in bringing back unpleasant memories, she gave comfort.

Taking Dakota's hand, Blake stood and helped her up from the bench. "Come on lazybones, we're not finished yet."

"I know you did not call me lazybones," she protested as he pulled toward the entranceway of the next room. Hand in hand they continued through the museum. This was one of the smaller rooms, everyone seemed to quietly flow through the room. Whispering, pointing and hurrying on to the next. They lingered by the glass displays.

Dakota turned and walked over to get a closer look at the selection of samurai swords and armor on display.

Blake took the opportunity to brush a strand of hair from Dakota's temple as she leaned in close to the glass to read the description. When she was finished she drew back but continued to direct her eyes toward the display. "I have an easy time picturing you as a warrior, Blake," she commented. "You have the same aura of confidence, courage and passion."

"If I'm a warrior, then that would make you my woman."

She gifted him with a sideways glance. "Or wife."

He moved closer to her. So close that she could feel his breath on her neck, the strength of his thigh next to hers. Yet, she pretended to be engrossed in the display. "It says here, that when the warrior returned from battle, his consort would great him at the door, lead him into the bathing chamber and remove his armaments. Then in an act of love, she would bath him before dressing him in fresh garments and serving him a traditional meal."

In her mind's eyes, Dakota imagined the scene and it wasn't the Japanese dolls performing the action, it was them. She pictured herself moving the sponge over his chest, neck and shoulders. Washing his thighs, legs and feet, then moving around to sponge his back and behind. Her body's reaction to the thoughts were swift and intense, the ache between her thighs weakened her knees. Dakota gratefully leaned against Blake. His arm slipped about her waist, his breath soft on her

Bound by Moonlight

skin. She could feel the length of his body pressing against her slender frame. She closed her eyes and drew a deep steadying breath.

"I know," Blake whispered.

She turned her head slowly and looked at him. "Know what?"

"That you want me inside you."

"How did you know?"

"Even if I couldn't see your face or hear the soft moan from your lips, I would know because the perfume of desire is on your skin."

Her cheeks, which were flushed from the daydream, grew hotter. Even the fact that they were having this conversation in public didn't dampen her arousal as she felt a stab of pure desire between her legs. "This isn't normal, Blake."

"But it's exciting, isn't it?" His breath hot in her ear.

"Yes," she murmured, surprised at his question. "I could never have imagined this...You."

He laughed low, took her hand and began to move away from the display. "Today is going to be a day of surprises, Dakota. That I promise."

A half hour later as they walked through the doorway, Blake and Dakota entered into the main hallway leading to other parts of the museum. He pulled her away from the center of traffic. "I don't know about you, but I could use a little sunlight and fresh air right now."

"Sounds good to me," she replied.

"How about we walk down the road and grab lunch at a local restaurant. I think I owe you lunch from keeping you in so many briefings."

Dakota punched him in the shoulder as they exited the building. "I thought you did that on purpose. Listening to economic consultants was about as exciting as the Ugandan President's opening address."

"I needed something nice to focus on, so I couldn't let you leave, now could I?"

"Yes, you could have. I could have just as easily been in the office with my head on the desk," she laughed as they exited the building.

The sidewalks were busy with busloads of uniformed children, and there was a swirl of excitement around them. Blake slipped his arm around her waist. "If it makes you feel better, the briefings put the rest of the team into a coma."

Dakota's body melted. The last few hours had, if anything, made Blake more irresistible. He was just as sexy relaxed as he was in a suit and tie. There was something about him and the way he held her that on that chilly sidewalk that made her feel delicate and cared for.

Making a mental decision not to think about Peter or the consequences of their public displays of affection, she snuggled under Blake's arm and lost herself in the beautiful balance of modern and old on the narrow careless streets of Tokyo.

Chapter 16

I don't know how you do it, woman. But I would rather have you under me than sitting here eating this outrageously expensive steak."

Something in his voice had her looking at him. And what Dakota saw there almost had her spilling wine down her dress. There was passion, perhaps a bit of possessiveness. But this time there was something new—a hint of the apprehension. She removed her hand from the top of the table, stuck it under the tabletop and placed it on his thigh. Maybe the combination of a perfect day, two glasses of wine and a handsome man, but she couldn't keep herself from wanting to touch or be touched by him.

His thigh muscle jumped underneath her palm, and her heart nearly leaped out of her chest before slowing to a steady pace. When he saw something he wanted, he reached out and took it. This was the very characteristic that attracted her to him. The same one that continued to bother her, more than she'd like to admit. But now with his show of apprehension, they seemed to have returned to something close to an equal footing and that small admission made her want him all the more.

Her fingers moved upward and rested atop his stiffened member, hesitated and then she slid her hand down in a heated stroke that had every nerve ending in his body standing at alert. With his eyes locked with hers, he rapidly calculated the length of time and the most expedient route to get them from the restaurant to the hotel. Then he still had to pay the check. She squeezed his leg lightly, then moved to cup his erection and he clenched his jaw.

Dakota's heavy-lidded gaze and sultry expression made him want to kiss her lips. "You are being a very bad girl, Dakota."

She boldly stared into his eyes, and just when Blake thought his need couldn't get more intense, it doubled.

His admiring gaze leisurely moved over her body, then moved up to her hair brushed it behind her ears in a casual fashion. She looked both like a seductress and a little girl at the same time. Her perfect bow of a mouth, soft cheeks and wide-eyed stare made her appear innocent. But after the other night, Blake knew would do everything in his power to be the last man to touch her.

"You did the same to me at the Taiko performance. Payback is horrible, isn't it?"

"Wait until we are alone," he growled.

Her smile widened. "Is that a threat?"

"No, it's a promise."

"Will you keep it?"

"Oh, yes."

He waved his hand and signaled to the waiter to bring them the check before returning his attention to Dakota.

Her hand had moved away, but the kneading of her fingertips continued to add fuel to the fire. "You are playing a dangerous game." His voice was deep with controlled passion.

Dakota's eyes lit up. "I like games, and I know you like them, too."

"I won't play unless we agree on the rules."

Her brow creased and the smile slipped from her lips. "I don't like rules, Blake"

"If it helps, these will be my rules."

"Then game over," she teased. "I don't want to play."

"Ahh, so the indomitable and intrepid Dakota Montgomery gives up that easily?" Blake pulled out his wallet and slipped the yen notes into a leather bill jacket.

"No. I just don't like to play by anyone's rules."

"Except your own, of course?"

She smiled as he stood, walked behind her chair and gently pulled it back. When Dakota stood she deliberately stepped back and pressed her rear against his front. She smiled brighter as the evidence of his arousal

Bound by Moonlight

strained against her buttocks. Patience was not a part of her nature, and she'd spent the day waiting for the night. Since their morning at the museum, her body had ached for his touch and she would wait no longer.

"Naturally."

"You think that you can control this thing between us?" Blake asked softly.

He reached out and caressed the side of her cheek, then trailed downward to brush the graceful curve of her neck. Her body of its own accord reacted and underneath her sweater, Dakota's nipples hardened.

Blake placed his hand on the curve of her back and led her outside. As soon as they passed the door, the diplomatic service agents made themselves visible and a car door opened. He helped her situate herself in the car, then he closed the door and went to the other side. Dakota reached over to place on her seat belt but Blake was faster. To the front passengers it looked innocent. To Dakota it was wicked as sin as his fingertips brushed across her breasts and his teeth closed over the soft flesh of her earlobe for a second, before he spoke. "Think that I let it play out on your terms, in your time, that you'll be able to direct how much you'll give and take?" He clicked the seatbelt into place. "If you play this game with me, if you come to my bed, you'd better be prepared to bet it all, because I will take nothing less."

His rules. Her life was a testament to breaking rules. Every assignment called for evaluating the truth, going against the status quo. And the time had long since passed when she'd stopped denying it. Duty to the truth was only a part of her commitment to the job. The adrenaline highs and sweetness of the award-winning expose that came with the assignments were as addictive as any drug.

Even with her attention divided between listening to Blake's words and feeling the heat brought from his touch, she could see the resolution in his expression, the automatic certainty of his words. She was used to guarding her emotions, making her decisions on a mixture of cool calculating logic as he did. But her cool logic was failing her and for that moment, Dakota wanted to be reckless, go against her own rules and be

150

reckless. There was nothing planned about the way his hand moved under her dress, nothing remotely chilly with the fingertips rubbing the stocking covered inside of her thigh.

Thankful of the dark glass partition between the front and back seats, Dakota bit her lip to remain silent and hung her head. When she looked over at Blake, his eyes were straight ahead and nothing seemed amiss. A ripple of disquiet flowed down her spine at the ease over which he controlled her body. Not one to play by the rules, she slid her hand from the armrest and trailed it higher on his thigh, her index finger tracing the crease between his thigh and groin. Her hand cupped him, and she felt his erection jump against the palm of her hand. He didn't quite manage to restrain his sharp indrawn breath. The indication on his response fired her own.

By the time, the car turned into the hotel's driveway, she was more than wet and ready. One of the hotel staff opened the door for her. Dakota kept herself still until Blake came to stand by her side, slid his arm around her waist. She looked neither right nor left, nor did she look anyone in the eye. It would have been impossible for her to conceal her emotions.

"We are being watched, Blake," she protested breathlessly as he guided her rapidly through the lobby and toward the elevator.

He glanced around, slowed his pace, and relaxed his grip somewhat. "I know." Reaching the elevator, she attempted to move away, but he held her in place while pressing the button impatiently.

"And we're supposed to maintain a professional relationship."

"After today, we both know that's not possible," he taunted, turning to face her with a wry grin. The doors opened and a family stepped out. Dakota stepped in and watched as Blake slid in his keycard and pressed the button to their floor. The doors slid shut, and she found herself pushed against the wall.

The fire she'd sparked at the end of dinner erupted as he crowded her against the wall of the elevator and took her lips again. His mouth demanded and took; his tongue pushed against her lips and encircled hers. And when his mouth left hers, Blake's lips cruised down the slender curve of her throat. His hands cupped her bottom and kneaded as her legs parted, allowing him to come closer. Her hand rested lightly on his hip, and her heavy lidded eyes took in the sight of his closely cropped head. He pulled away, leaving her panting. As his hips bucked and pressed against her, his tongue traced her throat, finding the furiously beating pulse. His teeth nipped her skin, causing Dakota to tip her head back, allowing him freer access. Her arms moved upward and her fingers clenched on his shoulders as her knees threatened to buckle.

"Blake, the elevator could stop...." Dakota's voice trailed off as he stoked his hand over her breast.

"It won't."

His mouth was hot, his unfathomable eyes were dark depths of desire that an unwise woman could drown in.

Her breath hitched as his finger moved, one excruciating inch at a time, to her throat. She didn't seem to be breathing at all as his finger traveled at a snail's pace to poise between her breasts.

For several heartbeats, all he did was stare at her breasts. And his look of lust and tenderness proved to her that Blake wouldn't be a man like any other, to share an intimate night and a breakfast goodbye. She wouldn't be able to dismiss him from her mind, or use her childhood love of Peter to trivialize the affair.

The elevator stopped. Still clenched in each other's arms, they made it into Blake's hotel suite and into his bedroom. Feeling as though she would burn up from the inside out, Dakota pulled off her sweater, unzipped her pants and let them fall to the floor. And somehow without touching her, he unhooked her bra. She lowered her arms, and it fell to the floor. She wouldn't have thought it possible, but his eyes darkened even further. Dakota looked down to follow his gaze.

Her breasts were high, round, the nipples pebbled to hardness. She watched as he bent his head and took one of her nipples into his mouth and lashed it with his tongue. It was simply too delicious. She whimpered and moved restless beneath his touch as she grew wetter. Closing her eyes. Dakota drew him closer, arched her back and laid her head on his shoulder. Never before had she felt such hot desire as was now speeding through her veins.

She tugged his shirt from his pants, then those hands were sliding up his sides. The feel of those muscles underneath her fingers released something primitive inside her. This was what she wanted, and yet it wasn't enough. Not nearly enough.

He reached down, sought the sensitive nub of flesh that was at the core of her womanhood. He played with it, slowly touching, teasing and coaxing her toward release. Tenderly he inserted his finger and her muscles gripped him. The volume of her moans increased, and a small orgasm rippled up her skin just from the touch of his hand.

"You are so tight," he whispered as his lips touched hers.

He released her breast, admired the sight of her turgid nipple, wet from his mouth, then switched his attention to its twin. Everything about Dakota obsessed him. From the tiny whimpers in her throat, the sent of her arousal to her flawless skin the color of amber..

Then his mouth found hers. Naked flesh pressed against flesh caused a riot of sensation. Control slipped and he pressed his mouth harder onto hers. Her hands clutched his biceps, her breast flattened against his chest. This wasn't their first coupling, not even their third or fourth. And still he couldn't get enough of her.

Oxygen clogged in his lungs. The crisp air-conditioned air seemed too thick to breathe.

It was several moments before he realized they hadn't turned on the lights. Several more before he could mange to lift his mouth from hers. He gently turned her face toward the window and smiled at her indrawn breath. Now she could see why he'd chosen these hotel suites. In a rare occasion, the full moon hung suspended in a starry sky behind Mt. Fuji.

"I have never seen anything this beautiful," she whispered.

The cool light of the moon bathed them both as he took in her face, the flush in her cheeks, the sultry scent of her, the swell in her lips from his kisses. "That makes two of us."

He slipped his tongue into her mouth, and she eagerly accepted it. While they had kissed many times before, this time was different. There was something compelling about laying in the moonlight. Something permanent. He broke the kiss and pulled her into his embrace, caressing her back. It was as if he couldn't touch her enough, couldn't hold her long enough. His hands cupped her bottom, and the satiny smooth texture of her skin, made him even harder.

Leaning forward, Dakota nipped at his shoulder hard enough to make him catch his breath, and the pain only increased his hunger, making him grow harder, then she massaged the slight sting with her tongue.

His hands on her hips, he moved and ran his finger over the outside of her clit and found her wet, swollen and waiting. He battled to not give into temptation. Not yet. Not until she was screaming out from the pleasure he gave her, moaning his name, crying. Not until he'd branded her as his own so that her flesh would allow no other man to lay a hand on her without the memory of him.

The thought of another man touching what was his had Blake clenching his jaw to battle back an irrational, jealous fury. A hint of it must have been reflected in his expression because when Dakota opened her eyes, she swallowed at the sight of him.

"Blake?"

He stroked away the fear in her voice with a gentle hand gliding down her back, pressed a deep hungry kiss on her mouth to prevent any further questions. They had an uncertain future, but they had the present. Now. Here. Tonight. And he would make it last until the last possible minute.

His chest tightening, he stared down at her, imprinting the picture she made with the moonlight at her back on his memory. Her earlier fears had faded, and the only emotion on her face was desire. He reached up and released her hair from its ponytail. The tangle of dark hair covered her bare shoulders, teased his fingertips. Her skin was the color of rich honey, inviting his kiss. With her curves promising heaven in her arms, she personified sex, wicked and seductive.

As if reading his thoughts, her lips tilted upward. With a deliberate stretch she placed the outside of her leg over his and leaned in closer to place her hand on his manhood.

He grabbed her waist and suckled her nipples. They were as hard as black diamonds. She ran her fingers over his hair and kissed his forehead as he took one of her bare breasts into his mouth. He heard her moaning and pushed on. He gently pushed her back on bed, covered in silken sheets and an oversized down comforter. He worked his way from her stomach to her thighs. He blew on the hairs and had to place his arm around her waist to keep Dakota from moving away.

"You liked that, didn't you?"

"Yes," she whimpered.

God she was beautiful. The moonlight streamed into the room, patterning the bed with slivers of light. He moved in closer and used his tongue to stimulate her clit while his left hand squeezed her breast. She moaned and screamed as her body bucked from the force of her orgasms. A pure masculine surge of satisfaction filled him. The sound of her passion erased every sense of civility he possessed. There would be nothing between them but this. The pleasure, the tension, the prelude to a glorious release.

She gripped his shoulders and tried to pull him up to her. He skimmed his mouth over her stomach and stopped to nuzzle her breasts. Blake loved the way they fit in his mouth, hungered for the taste.

Dakota's whimper of frustration drew a smile to his face.

"Now, Blake. Finish this."

He studied her, brushing her hair from her face. "Wait." He nuzzled her smooth skin on the back of her head, his hand stoking her mound, toying with her clit. Her body shuddered and bucked beneath him as he parted her slick folds, penetrated her with one stroke of his finger. Her heels dug into the bed, her back arched. She was tight and quivering around his finger. He pulled out and moved in using the tip of his thumb to stimulate the sensitive nub. Her nails dug into his shoulder as she went wild beneath him. And the need to possess her cut though him like a blade.

Bound by Moonlight

Blake levered himself up enough to reach over, opened the drawer on the nightstand, and took out one of the foil-lined packets. As he unwrapped the condom, she reached down covered his manhood with her hand and gently squeezed. His hips jerked involuntarily, one hand bracing himself with the bed. She reached out and took the condom from his nerveless fingers. It took every bit of willpower he possessed to allow Dakota to cover the latex over his length, with painful slowness.

And when she'd completed her task, he grabbed her arms and positioned them above her head, locking his other hand around her wrist. He nestled himself between her legs, fit himself intimately to the apex of her thighs. Her hips surged upward under his, eager and demanding. He rubbed his lips against her neck and sucked the spot above her pulse.

"Please, Blake!"

Having reached the point where he could not hold back without spilling his seed, he slid inside her with one hard thrust.

Dakota bucked beneath him, body shuddering, her chest rising off the bed as her hand struggled to break free from his grasp. When her legs wrapped around his hips, he couldn't think, couldn't breathe. She was tight as a fist around him. The sensation of her inner muscles clenching around him felt too good. Each of her movements pulled him deeper inside her. Placing his weight on his arms, he surged against her in a slow shallow rhythm.

The bite of her nails on his shoulders and the feel of her heels pressing into his thighs urged him deeper. Faster. Her legs climbed to his hips and clasped around his waist. He kissed her deep and wet, sucked the air from her mouth and swallowed her moans. They moved together, each pressing the other. He watched her eyes go blind as her female muscles contracted in spasms around his male muscle. And when her body went taut beneath him and her inner walls grew tight around him, he hammered himself into her. Only when he swallowed her cry of pleasure did he allow himself to let go. And when he followed her over the edge, all he heard was the echo of her name from his lips.

He collapsed on top of her, shuddering though an orgasm unlike anything he'd ever known. Barely able to move, he managed to twist to

156

the side and wrap his arms around her supine body and pulled her to him in a tender embrace. Blake buried his face in her neck and breathed as his pulse began slow. For the next few minutes, he stared at the shadow of her face. And his heart gave voice to what his soul seemed to have known since the first time he set eyes on the woman in his arms.

Blake Holland had finally fallen in love.

Dakota woke to the sharp sound of her name being called. She yawned, then wiped the sleep from her eyes.

"Shower and get dressed," Blake said.

She rubbed her eyes again, turned over and winced at the delicate soreness between her thighs.

Her mind still hazed by sleep and satiated by their making love not just once but three times last night, she questioned. "What?"

"I need you to shower, get dressed and pack a bag."

"Why?"

"Our train leaves in four hours."

Dakota blinked and levered herself up in bed. As soon as she could focus on Blake, her body tensed. He was fully dressed in black trousers and a chestnut-colored turtleneck sweater. "I'm not going anywhere without a destination."

"Trust me, Dakota. I promise you'll enjoy it."

Blake sat down, then leaned over until his face was mere inches from hers. He barely resembled the passionate man she'd shared a bed with last night. Eyes that had burned her soul, sat cold and empty, lips that had covered her flesh in delicate licks and kisses, pulled into a thin line. His hand came up and Dakota barely managed to keep herself from scooting away. It felt as though she were being touched by a stranger.

Their eyes locked, and she held still. He ran his fingers though her hair, then traced the curve of her cheek with his index finger. "I need for you to trust me." His voice softened.

Bound by Moonlight

Dakota swallowed and worked hard to speak past the lump in her throat. "I want to."

He inhaled deeply. "When I was a five years old, my mother started to gain weight. I remember the evening she came home from work and laid down in her bed. I was hungry and when I walked into her tiny bedroom to ask about supper, she started to scream." He closed his eyes and Dakota's heart stopped. His voice lowered as he continued. "There was blood on the sheets. She stopped screaming and began to moan. I stood in the doorway and peed in my pants. I couldn't move. She screamed at me to go next door to the Brown's house and fetch Lynn. I still couldn't move. And she screamed again, the high-pitched sound I'd only heard once before when my uncle had shot his lame mutt. So I ran out the house without my shoes and no coat in the middle of winter. I ran a quarter of a mile down a muddy road. The neighbor's wife came and helped my mother have the baby. I watched my little sister come into the world, and I remember praying to God not to take my mother away. I actually held her afterwards. And while my mother passed out, the neighbor's wife cleaned up and shook her head saying it was a shame that my mother was a harlot. She called my sister a pretty little bastard child."

Blake's shoulders slumped as if a great burden had all of a sudden come crashing down. "My mother made the mistake of falling in love with a traveling salesman when she was only seventeen. She had never left the town she'd grown up in, and when he offered to show her the world, she packed a bag and didn't look back. But less than a year later, she came back with the same bag. Moved into a cabin on my Uncle Ray's property and had me. When my father came back years later and stayed for a summer, my sister was conceived. Then he disappeared. I thought he was dead. Later, I wished he was dead. Every day of our lives my sister, Caroline and I were ridiculed. My mother never sat in the front row of the church. I was eleven when I found out the man I called my father had another family in Philadelphia. He had three other children, a wife, a big brick house and a shiny Ford." His voice broke under the strain of emotion.

158

Knowing how much this was costing him, Dakota didn't say a word but gently took him into her arms and rested his head against her shoulder.

"My mother knew about his other life, yet she still loved him." The raw emotion of the statement rendered his voice hoarse.

Dakota closed her eyes to keep in the hot wetness of tears from escaping. His pain tore her heart, and she knew as sure as she knew her own name that Blake had never spoken of his life to anyone. "It's going to be all right, I promise."

He seemed to draw strength from her words and continued in a monotone voice. "My mother died when I was fourteen. Her family took my sister and I in and raised us as best they could. We both won scholarships to attend college. She's married to a good man, and she's due to have my first nephew in five months. I've fought hard to get to where I am, Dakota. And I did it all out of spite. I wanted to show that son-of-a-bitch father of mine that Lilly Holland's son was a survivor. I wanted to show him and the small-minded bigots who called us bastards that we were too good for them. And I always thought it would be enough."

He paused for several heartbeats; Dakota remained silent and stroked his back. "But it's not enough," she surmised.

Blake gently guided her face toward his own. "No. Just like last night wasn't enough. I dreamed of you last night, woke up wanting you. I want you now, and the thought of being in a room with you and other people makes me crazy. The idea of seeing you talk to another man awakens a rage I can't control."

"Blake, how can we just disappear on the eve of the trade conference?"

"My team has everything under control, and we're still a week from the opening session. Two days, Dakota. Give me enough time to get a handle on whatever this is between us."

There was but one response and they both knew it. As much as he didn't understand what was happening to the both of them, she didn't either. She wasn't naïve enough to think she could make love and walk away. Her teenaged puppy love for Peter seemed a pale and colorless emotion when compared to the whirlwind of feelings just the mere sight of Blake conjured up.

She sat forward and buried her face in his neck. "I'll go," she whispered.

Chapter 17

Hours later, Blake woke as the car pulled into Tokyo Station. Glancing over he saw Dakota's eyes were closed and her lips curled upward as if she were smiling at something that only she could see. He could only suspect what, and the suspicion didn't reassure him. His ego wouldn't let him think that the smile on her lips could be for anyone other than himself, but he wasn't a complete fool. Peter O'Connor was a threat he couldn't ignore. For the moment Dakota was his completely, but the closer it came to the conference opening and the further their investigations of O'Connor's possible espionage activities progressed, things would get worse. And there wasn't a damn thing he could do about it.

Inwardly he sighed. She was so beautiful. As much as Blake simply lusted after her, he gazed at her with much more complicated emotions: desire, anger, warmth and tenderness. With her he could be himself; with others he could not. Never in a million years could he have imagined he would share his childhood secrets with any woman, much less a journalist.

The car pulled in front of the Tokyo Station. He waited until the diplomatic security agents had obtained their luggage, then he exited the car. He walked to the other side and opened the car door; Dakota took his hand without prompting. Even at one o'clock in the afternoon, they had to wait for a break in the steady flow of human traffic. The agents preceded them onto the walkway. Although he'd seen the station in photographs, Blake couldn't help but pause to take in the magnificent red-brick building, which was reminiscent of a train station he'd viewed in Amsterdam's main station.

"Blake?" Dakota's softly voice query pulled him from his thoughts. He pulled her closer, and one glance made him acutely aware of the

Bound by Moonlight

attention their small group was receiving from Japanese commuters. Attention was the last thing Blake wanted. They entered through the door, and he followed Agent Dawson through the crowded interior court- yard toward the Tokaido bullet train platform. Like the street outside, the station was filled with people. Confident in the Japanese obsession with precision, within thirty minutes, they would be en route to the country- side of Fuji aboard a bullet train.

"I've never been here before," Dakota said.

Blake looked down into her unadorned face. The lack of artifice made her look all the more natural and desirable to him. Her lips still looked tender from his kisses. "Me either," he replied.

Her lips curled upward and his heart warmed. "Looks like we're both moving into unknown territory, huh?"

Blake nodded while keeping one eye on her and the other paying attention to where they were going. The cacophony of voices and stream of Japanese female voices over the loudspeaker increased his excitement. "Completely." He grinned.

"Now that we're at the station, you have a promise to keep," Dakota said.

His brow furrowed, and then the memory surfaced. He'd wanted to surprise her with their destination, and refused to answer her questions. The sight of Dakota's completely nude body bathed in the warm purples and oranges of the morning sunrise had made him lose all thought and willpower. He'd never spoken about his childhood to anyone, but seeing her lying there asleep, he knew he'd never give her up. And having her in his life, having her in his bed, required giving her his trust.

He tampered down his internal musing and focused on the present. "Shizuoka."

"Shi-zu-o- ka," Dakota repeated sounding out the word. "Why does it sound so familiar?"

"It's a region west of Tokyo and is home to a world famous view."

Her eyes sparkled and Blake knew the exact second that her mind figured out his destination.

"Mt. Fuji."

162

"And I just thought you were a local reporter," he teased.

One of his two security agents signaled. "Sir, please step back. The train is about to arrive. Once it stops and the doors open we'll lead you to the seats."

He nodded and moved accordingly. His focus returned to Dakota's face, but he found her attention directed elsewhere. Catching the glimpse of movement out the corner of his eyes, he glanced down the track.

Blake had never considered himself to be a technologically savvy. Well-versed in the cutting edge tools used in the business world, he fully appreciated items like antique cars or a Mont Blanc pen. Yet, the *shinkansen* was striking; with a long, pointed needle nose more like that of a supersonic plane than a conventional high-speed train.

He turned and experienced more pleasure just looking at the awe on Dakota's face.

"I wish they'd had these around when I was younger. It always took two days to get home when I took the train," she quipped.

Blake laughed and as the door stopped exactly in front of them. One of the agents picked up their luggage and stepped on the train.

"Ready, for another first?" Blake asked. Nothing in the world seemed to match the happiness he drew from the look in Dakota's eyes.

"Anytime, Holland. Lead the way."

Dakota stepped into the entranceway, turned right and followed Blake into a narrow corridor. She'd expected the inside of the train to resemble any modern airliner with inward-curving sides and rounded windows. But as he led her through another doorway, her eyes widened in surprise. The space was structured like a private meeting room with a table in the middle, a sofa with pillows on one side and two seats on the other. The cabin also had a flat screen television displaying the weather that sat on one of the walls, a mini fridge under the table and computer data port sat on top.

Blake placed Dakota next to the window, then sat back as the train began to slowly move away from the track and smoothly accelerate out of the station. Even as the train hit high speeds, it barely swayed.

"This is incredible, Blake." Dakota leaned close to the window. And he smiled at the sight of her nose so close to the glass. Knowing that she had traveled the world, her excitement added to his own excitement. As the train swung south heading toward Yokohama, he gathered her into his arms, and as they raced through the city of Tokyo, he let himself relax.

"Blake?" Dakota broke the silence.

"Hmm."

"Will the diplomatic security agents be joining us?"

"No, they have their own cabin. This is a specially made railcar that high-level Japanese government officials use. The entrance door will remain locked until we reach our destination."

Dakota stood and moved to the cabin door. Her hand rested on the lock. "So it's okay if I lock our door?"

"You can do anything you want, beautiful."

Her eyes darkened. "Anything?"

Blake's body jumped at the look of desire on her face. "Anything."

She slid the bolt into place, and then walked over to the window and drew the curtains. "When I was in the shower this morning, I thought about being with you on a train for hours. How I would have to sit next to you without touching you." She slipped out of her shoes and walked toward him. "Without kissing you." She leaned down, and taking his face between her hands, began to kiss him. Her kisses touched his mouth, his eyelids and his face. Blake remained with his eyes closed and enjoyed every one of them.

When she pulled away, he began to open his eyes, she gently brushed her thumbs over them.

"No, keep your eyes closed for me," she whispered, her breath hot in his ear. "I just want you to feel."

She pulled away, and he heard the sound of clothing rustling and hitting the floor.

"I don't know if I can keep my eyes closed, Dakota. Especially if you're stripping."

She laughed, and the husky sound filled the cabin. He damn near jumped out of his skin, when Dakota placed both hands on his shoulders and straddled his lap,

"Now this is more like it," he murmured. He felt the warmth of her body through his shirt, the soft fullness of her breasts against his chest...and the more urgent heat of something even more delectable, pressed against the hardening in his pants.

"Is it?" Dakota whispered against his lips before kissing him.

Blake moved his head forward, wrapped his arms around her, both hands tracing the soft line of her back as he leaned into the kiss, their mouths parting, tongues darting in and tasting each other. His hands slid over her sweater and found purchase on her naked bottom.

"I want you inside me, Blake Holland," she whispered again, breathing the words into their kiss. "I want to ride you like a stallion and take your moans into my mouth."

Blake pulled his head back, breaking their kiss, and struggled to breathe... and Dakota slid back far enough to escape his grasp. He felt her nimble fingers catch hold of the buckle on the slender leather belt he wore. She tugged it apart easily, then slipped the top button on his jeans open as well...yanking the zipper down as quickly as she could.

He struggled not to open his eyes while she did this, his hands gentle on her back, allowing her to take the lead...but when her hands slipped inside his pants and closed over his straining erection, he opened his eyes and bit his bottom lip, stifling the ragged groan that threatened to escape his throat.

"No peeking," Dakota whispered.

"You ask too much," Blake replied, his voice ragged. Reaching out he pushed up underneath her sweater, he began to fondle her breasts while she caressed his manhood. He groaned as her delicate hands squeezed him. She gasped when he pinched her nipples, leaning forward, he placed his mouth against the slender curve of her neck and sucked.

When her fingers tightened and the scent of her arousal filled his sense, Blake knew he couldn't take any more. He slid his hands out from underneath her sweater and grasped her by the waist. What he wanted more than anything else has to plunge into her, but he stopped. He needed to protect her.

"My wallet…" he managed to say through gritted teeth.

Very quickly, he watched as she pulled out his wallet, then a foil wrapped condom. She sheathed his hardness, and before he could even take another breath, she began to lower herself slowly, slowly impaling herself upon his manhood until he was fully inside. Dakota sighed as their two bodies were joined so perfectly.

She wrapped her arms about his neck and whispered hot words in his ears as her teeth nipped the delicate rim. Her body tingled and she could actually feel him swelling within her. Instinctually, she tightened her muscles around him. His harsh groan only intensified her pleasure. "I love the feel of you inside of me, Blake. You fill me."

She wanted to say more but couldn't. Dakota swallowed her words as Blake's hands locked around her waist, lifted her up and with one swift thrust he plunged himself back inside her tight, slick heat. Dakota tossed her head, a soft, guttural cry escaping from her lips as Blake withdrew and pulled her down again. He moved with a leisurely fashion, lifting her and drawing himself almost out, and then plunging back with a harsh intensity.

Dakota struggled to gain some small measure of control and failed as she shuddered with desire. "Come for me, Dakota," he murmured low against her ear and quickened the pace thrusting harder and harder.

She buried her face in the curve of his neck as he took his shirt between her teeth to muffle her cries as the world exploded and pleasure spiraled through her body. Blake continued to move within her as her muscle clenched and unclenched bringing him to his own climax, and then seconds later as her body lay limp in his arms, Blake struggled to breathe.

He felt the motion of the train and fought against the relentless urge to sleep. "Dakota."

"Hmm?"

A small smile crept over his face. She sounded as if she were drunk or high on drugs. Then again, that was exactly how he felt. "You are amazing."

"As are you, Blake." She lifted her head from his shoulder and kissed his mouth tenderly. "I have a favor to ask."

"Anything."

"Can we have this car on the way back?"

"Minx." He laughed out load and pulled her to him. "We've got about two more hours until we arrive. We had better make the most of that time."

The next evening, Dakota allowed her head to sink back against the rim of the deep Japanese bathtub, relishing the warmth of the water as it lapped over her skin. There was a pervasive chill to the air around her…it was windy outside and the multi windowed bathing room was by far the least insulated area in the private suite. But having grown up in a region that suffered from the worst winters in the country, Dakota was more than comfortable with Japan's version of a cold night.

She sighed and closed her eyes, her hands dangling over the sides of the tub as her thoughts drifted pleasantly. Just as she'd expected, her father had called that morning before Dakota and Blake had managed to get out of bed. Her lips turned upward. It had been nearly impossible not to giggle as he'd tickled her back and touched her in her most sensitive places. Dakota was sure her happiness must have come through the phone line. And for her father, that was all that mattered.

For now only Blake mattered, Dakota thought lazily, a slight smile spreading across her face as she idly shifted her body in the warm water. The smile slipped from her lips as she remembered she still needed to tell him the truth about her getting "lost" on the subway. Guilt stabbed her heart because Blake had been very explicit in his orders that she not see Nobu. In light of his own personal confessions before they left Tokyo,

Bound by Moonlight

she had to tell him the truth. Only she didn't want to ruin this beautiful trip. Dakota chewed on her bottom lip, and then sat back in the tub. She would tell him during the train ride back, that way he would be forced to listen, and she would be able to explain why she did what she did.

Having come to that decision, Dakota relaxed. Soon he would walk through the door and join her. She'd made sure he saw her undress and enter into the bathing room…the handsome man was never one to turn down an invitation. Not to mention that they'd spent the day hiking around the base of Mt. Fuji and a quick shower they'd taken immediately after returning to the cabin would not be enough to sooth the soreness of his muscles.

She leaned back again with her eyes closed and began to idly soap her skin, the restless sound of the wind outside muffled even the soft sound of water splashing.

And then a different scent wafted by, deep and woodsy at the same time as it mixed subtly with the scent of her soap. Blake.

The soft sound of a footstep, barely heard against the stone floor, made her smile return. Dakota lifted the sponge and began to soap her breasts, not bothering to open her eyes and fix them on her admirer.

"I missed you," she laughed softly.

"You abandoned me." The soft, distinctive bass of his voice felt like a caress, and Dakota raised her eyes slowly, letting her gaze settle on the tall, handsome man standing in the bath doorway. A slow smile spread across his face, looking both handsome and charmingly boyish as he paused there, one hand poised on the sliding door, the other hanging by his side with mobile phone between his fingers.

"I knew you would come," she said, turning back to her bath, but not before giving him a teasing look from the corner of her eye.

"Did you now?"

Her gentle laugh seemed to coax him, and he left the doorway and crossed the room to the small bathing stool, sitting across from the foot of the tub against the near wall. Without taking his eyes from her, Blake sat in the chair.

168

"I would have thought you'd be finished by now," he commented, raising his eyebrows and grinning at her from as he stretched his legs out and leaned back against the wall. "You know...since we're expected at dinner soon."

She raised one shapely leg from the soapy water, negligently running her sponge over the line of her thigh. "I'm not really hungry yet," she said. "And I really enjoyed the time we spent together today. It feels so nice having alone time."

"Would you like me to go?"

She laughed and raised her eyes to his. "What do you think?"

Blake grinned, and even if she hadn't been hot from the bathwater, the sheer male appreciation in his gaze would have warmed her. "I think I'm enjoying the view a little too much to go to dinner alone."

Dakota laughed. She sat up in the tub, her upswept hair falling down to frame her face in gentle curls. "Do you only plan to watch, Blake?" she asked teasingly. "Or did you have something else in mind?"

His brow rose. "That depends, beautiful."

"On what?" She began soaping her shoulders, deliberately graceful, alluring...holding her arms out one at a time as she ran the sponge over her skin, keeping one eye on Blake and his reaction.

"On how long you're planning on staying in the bath."

Dakota laughed again, her eyes nearly dancing...and she rinsed off her sponge, ridding it of soap, and then loading it up with water again, which she squeezed over her breasts and shoulders, the soap running off her skin in bubbly rivulets. Blake said nothing, but remained smiling as he watched her finish her bath.

"Your mobile phone rang earlier," he said after a moment. He said it casually, studying the design patterns of the wooden beams in the ceiling as if mentioning it in passing...but Dakota didn't miss the slight uplift in his words, as if he were testing her, seeking some sort of reaction. "Were you expecting a phone call?"

"Maybe, maybe not." Dakota finished rinsing the soap from her body, then lifted her hand and let the sponge drop into the water with a soft splash. "Why? Are you worried?"

"Not about you," Blake replied. "Since O'Conner is expected to be in Tokyo soon and I don't want him getting any ideas now that you're grown up."

"What would it matter?" she said. She curled her fingers around the sides of the tub and stood up with a slosh, noting with a trace of inner gratification the way his eyes abruptly moved to her body. Water ran down her stomach, over her legs. She reached for the towel folded neatly on the small stand next to the tub, shaking it out and beginning to pat herself dry.

"You and I have no claims on one another," she continued, her tone serious, "if Peter were to magically appear and declare that he sees me as a woman and not as a sister, would that bother you?"

His eyes narrowed. "Hell, yes. I don't even want to think about that," Blake replied with a soft growl. "I don't share...and like it or not Dakota, you are mine."

Dakota stepped out of the tub onto the fluffy mat beside it, bending to dry off her legs, then she straightened again and slipped the towel behind her back, drying off her bottom with a cute little shimmy-shake. Her eyes were alight, reflecting the flames of the candles dotting the room, the snow falling past the night-darkened windows behind her creating a backdrop that set off her bath-warmed skin to lovely advantage.

"Does it ever worry you, Blake," she asked, stepping gracefully across the floor and approaching him where he sat. "That this passion between us isn't real? That maybe when this is all over, this connection will disappear?"

"Never." Blake didn't look worried at all. His handsome face bore a look of deep interest instead, his obsidian eyes roaming over her body as she came closer. Dakota held the towel draped over her shoulders like a wrap, clasping it together in front of her breasts as she came closer and stopped just inside the space between his parted legs. His slow gaze traced up her body to her face, locking eyes with her in an expectant silence.

"Like what you see?" She arched a lovely eyebrow.

"Only if I could see a little more of you," he replied, the slow spark of lust in his eyes unmistakable as he spread his knees a little wider, allowing Dakota to take another step into his regard.

"And are you planning on doing something about it?" she asked.

"Oh, yes." He reached forward and covered her hands with his, gently tugging the towel free of her hands. She relented to him with little more than a pleased sound as he pulled the terry material away from her breasts and allowed it to fall unheeded to the floor. Blake's hands closed over hers once more, warm and smooth, and she allowed him to pull her closer, her breasts brushing against his lips gently.

"Tease…" he murmured. She closed her eyes, lifting her hands and interlacing her fingers behind his neck, delighting in its softness as his hands slipped around her waist. Blake pulled her even closer, burying his face between her breasts and inhaling the fragrance of her skin, his strong fingers slipping over the small of her back and over the curve of her bottom with leisurely enjoyment.

A ragged sigh escaped him. "Do you know what you do to me?"

Dakota opened her eyes again and looked down into his face, brushing against her breasts as he pressed a private kiss to her skin. "No…tell me," she said softly.

"May I show you instead?" He moved his hand and gently cupped her breast, pulling his head away from her long enough to look up and catch her gaze…then he slowly guided the cocoa-tinted nipple into his mouth. Dakota hissed in her breath lightly, Blake's other hand tightening on her behind, squeezing the round flesh…then he pulled her closer, so close she had to put one hand on his shoulder to steady herself against his chest. The shirt he wore felt wonderfully soft against her skin.

Blake sucked her nipple gently, his eyes still holding hers, then he gripped it lightly between his teeth, teasing the tip with a series of butterfly-light flutters of his tongue.

"Lord…" she whispered. With her body turned slightly and one thigh pressed against his groin, she felt his muscles jump there as she lightly skimmed her long nails up the back of his neck.

Bound by Moonlight

Dakota pulled away from him slightly, and he made a small sound of disappointment...but she only stepped away long enough to guide his legs together, then place her hands on his shoulders and straddle his lap. A shiver of pleasure ran through her at the feel of his jeans rubbing roughly against the skin of her bottom and thighs. Blake was also more than content with the change in position...he laughed and wrapped his lean, muscled arms around her slender waist, pulling her close enough to leave her wriggling with delight against the hardening mound in the crotch of his jeans.

"So nice," he murmured. He could feel the warmth of her body through his shirt, the soft fullness of her breasts against his chest, the more urgent heat of something even more delectable pressed against the flatness of his stomach.

"Is it?" Dakota leaned close to his face, catching it between her palms as she bent her head and pressed a slow, lingering kiss against his lips. Blake closed his eyes, both hands tracing the soft line of her back as he leaned into the kiss, their mouths parting, tongues darting in and tasting each other. Dakota gently moved her hips against his, rubbing against his burgeoning erection through his jeans.

"I want you inside me, Blake Holland," she whispered. "Now."

Blake pulled his head back, breaking their kiss. Dakota slid back far enough to reach between their bodies, her nimble fingers catching hold of the buckle of his leather belt. She tugged it apart easily, then slipped the top button on his jeans open as well...yanking the zipper down as quickly as she could. Blake watched her face while she did this, his hands gentle on her back, allowing her to take the lead this time...but when her hands slipped inside his jeans and closed over his straining erection, he closed his eyes and bit his bottom lip, stifling the ragged groan that threatened to escape his throat.

"Oh, beautiful..." Blake groaned.

Dakota freed his standing flesh, almost ridiculously delighted, as always, by the sight of him and the feel of him in her hand. She curled her fingers about it, squeezing it slightly, and her eyes half-lidded with

172

anxious desire as she watched the painful march of exquisite emotion across Blake's face.

She wanted nothing more than to have him naked inside of her and to feel his seed hot against her womb, but commonsense reared its head. Leaning to the side, she dug into his pants pocket until she found the foil treasure she sought. It took her less than a minute to put it on him. Dakota rested her weight on the balls of her feet, lifting herself slightly. Blake shifted himself a little underneath her as she slowly guided him between her legs.

Blake's hands slid down her back again, the fingers curling, digging into the swell of her buttocks, and he spread her cheeks apart as she lowered herself. Her thighs parted and the head of his penis brushed against her inner folds. Just that feather-light touch made her squeeze her eyes tightly shout and give a breathless, shattered moan. His penis slipped along the hot track between her legs, warm and slippery with her juices...then Blake pulled her hips toward him, startling a cry from Dakota's lips as he slid inside her with a single graceful thrust.

"Oh Blake..." Dakota let her forehead fall against his shoulder, her eyes still closed as her chest rose and fell in hard little breaths. His lips were close to her ear, his breathing harsh and raspy...and she moaned again as he ground his hips against hers, the feel of his erection inside her, coupled with the roughness of his jeans still rubbing against her thighs.

They remained that way for a moment, neither of them really moving, joined together as she sat straddling his lap...then holding his head in her hands, her slender fingers gripping his shoulders, she kissed him again, catching his bottom lip between her teeth and sucking it as she slowly began to move against him.

The friction of him sliding out of her, then back in...Blake made a soft, strangled sound, his fingers caressing her back, and she gasped and opened her eyes as she felt his mouth on her breast. The touch was unexpected, and undeniably sensual. She threw her head back, soft curls of hair tumbling down her back, her breasts thrust out in front of her where they bounced gently with her slow, hypnotic grinding of her hips against his.

Dakota matched his steady thrusts with her own as their flesh connected audibly. Her moans had dissolved into soft, gasping cries, punctuated with every slam of him inside her, her thighs feeling slick with her own wetness.

So close... so close...

Dakota closed her eyes as it hit her, an orgasm that felt like waves of flame.

She trembled violently, crying out with an almost painful ecstasy. Blake's head was thrown back, the cords of his neck standing out visibly as he groaned through clenched teeth at the ceiling. Seconds later he released her legs, sinking back against her as they joined together, arms wrapping around each other as he hid his face against her shoulder, a long, trembling groan escaping his lips.

"Love you..." Blake's hands left her bottom, and he wrapped his arms tightly around her waist, supporting her as she leaned back farther and he climaxed. And then as they lay seated, silence crept back into the room, and a breath of frigid wind rattled against the window, the only sounds in the room besides the soft, slowing pants of their breath. Dakota lifted a hand and gently touched Blake's face tenderly, stroking it with her fingers so he shivered again beneath her touch.

"I love you, Blake," she whispered softly. "I feel that I always will, no matter what happens between us."

"Nothing will take you away from me, Dakota. I won't allow it."

She felt him turn his head slightly, and he kissed her skin just above the breast, allowing his lips to linger there, then he raised himself slowly on his elbows, cradling her head between as he looked into her half-lidded, contented gaze.

Her eyes searched his. "What is it?"

"Nothing, baby. I just love looking at you."

She moved her behind a little, and then smiled. "Would you mind looking at me in bed? This floor is a little hard."

Blake laughed and levered himself up, and then Dakota. As they moved naked from the bathing room to the bedroom, the light of the moon, a peace he'd never known washed over him. And he prayed it would last.

Chapter 18

The next morning as sunlight began to trickle into the room, Dakota lay sprawled across Blake, her body lax and soft after their last bout of lovemaking. He was aware the moment he'd awoke, but he kept his eyes closed and continued to enjoy lightly stroking her back, the ample curves of her bottom. But his mind wasn't on the teasing feel of her hair against his chest. Something far heavier weighed on it.

"I could arrange for you to join my staff permanently in an analyst capacity," he said more bluntly than he'd intended. He felt her body tense and increased his massage. "You may come and go to any country or assignment you want. You will have more than adequate compensation and benefits."

Her voice, when it came, was expressionless. "I already possess those things."

"You've been lucky Dakota. It's only a matter of time until you're caught up in something that could get you killed," he said quietly. His eyes focused on the ceiling. "If not by the criminals you seek to interview, then by some corrupt official with enough power to stop you. You could end up in some foreign prison or dead. Take my offer and you'll have protection."

She tried to move away from him, but his arms tightened, locking her in place.

"It's my life." The words were hard, but with a note of uncertainty. "I know you can't understand, but this is something I need to do."

Rolling her to her back, he asked, "Have you thought about it? I've read your files from cover to cover, Dakota. You've barely escaped death too many times to think you're invincible. Do you really want to continue to take those chances? Your father needs you."

"Is this really about me, Blake?" Her hand rose up to cup his jaw and her words when they came, were spoken in a soft whisper. "Is this about my needs or yours?"

The simple question set loose a firestorm of doubts. He rolled away from her, filled with a futile anger. In truth, he didn't care about her father. He wanted her with him at all times. If he could not have that, then he would at least be able to have her protected. Deep within the guarded place of his heart, Dakota's image resided with his mother and sister. And once he loved, he never let go and unlike his father, he would guard this woman to his dying breath.

Getting out of bed, he pulled on his robe, closed the rice paper screen, and sat in the chair next to the bed. Without a word, he stared at her lying in the bed, half covered with a white sheet. It had to be the most beautiful thing he'd seen in his life. He struggled with the possibility that after they the trade conference ended, she could leave him or be injured on an assignment.

The phone rang, interrupting him. He reached over to the nightstand and glanced at the caller ID. The increasing familiar number of the Tokyo Embassy flashed across the screen. He answered, fully expecting to hear his assistant on the other end. The last person he expected to hear from was Reynolds, the diplomatic security bureau chief.

The conversation was brief. Long after it ended, Blake found himself looking at the phone, swallowing back wave after wave of erratic emotion.

"Blake, is something wrong?"

He felt Dakota's hand on his thigh and his jaw clenched, even as he formulated his response. "It's O'Conner," he said grimly. "The senator arrived in Japan last night."

After they'd both gotten out of bed and dressed. Neither spoke as the impact of Blake's announcement sat like an elephant in the middle of the room. Instead of talking about Peter, she'd thrown on her coat and left him as he sat at the desk, staring intently at his laptop. Now as she slipped into the suite via a sliding door, Blake stood in front of the open window, hands at his side, waiting.

Her teeth nibbled on her lips as her eyes traced over the broad shoulders down his back and over his muscular legs. Something about the way he stared out into the country landscape softened her resolve to be utterly casual. For a moment before he'd become aware of her presence, she'd seen underneath his veneers of confidence for a second time. And the sight of him vulnerable made her love him even more.

It hadn't taken her long to recognize the look in his eyes, for she'd seen it often in her reflection in the mirror as she moved from one hotel to another. Although she never would have fathomed it; Blake Holland was no stranger to loneliness. Dakota willed her legs to slowly cross the room to stand beside him.

As if captivated by the falling snowflakes, they turned toward one another and when his hand rose to stroke the side of her face, she gently nuzzled his palm. He pulled her to him and held her tight within the circle of his arms. The logical part of her mind knew she should have spoken and reminded him that they needed to talk about Peter, but her traitorous body warmed to his touch and her lips would not open, her mouth would not speak.

In the silence of the cabin suite, all she could hear was the sound of their breathing. Several moments passed before he spoke to her softly. "I have never needed anything more, than I needed you in my arms right now. Thank you."

More tender words had never been spoken to her. Dakota relaxed into his embrace. She inhaled his cologne and was drunk in the masculine scent. Turning her cheek, she smiled as he rested his chin atop her head and they both stared out at the falling snow. For the first time in her life, Dakota caught a glimpse of what really was to know true love.

Sweet jasmine. Dakota's signature scent wrapped around Blake like a silken blanket later that night. Slipping into the sheets, he snuggled her body against his and pulled the comforter up to him. Just the touch of her soft skin soothed him. He placed his arm around her waist and gently rubbed her stomach. Drained from the hour-long conference call, his body relaxed even as his mind continued to dwell on the latest piece of information regarding Senator O'Connor. Thanks to some well-placed wire taps, they'd discovered what Nobu had on the Senator. Blake sighed inwardly and buried his face in Dakota's neck. All of his anger toward O'Connor vanished. The man had been faced with an impossible situation: stand by and see the mother of his child and his son murdered or betray his country. Blake stoked a thumb against the soft swell of Dakota's belly and imagined his seed growing within her, pictured his son nursing from the breasts he himself loved to suckle.

His eyes closed and he soon matched his breathing to the woman he loved. Dakota would want to know, but seeing her peaceful face, made up his mind he would tell her. But the talk would wait until the morning...

Someone was in their bedroom.

From one second to the next, the thought woke Dakota from sleep. She held herself completely still and eased her eyes open. The light of a flashlight and the sound of moving feet over the tatami floor sent a wave fear so strong it cut off the air to her throat. Moving toward the edge of the bed, she opened her eyes and inhaled sharply at the sight of a shadow looming over her. She opened her mouth to scream and a leather-clad hand clamped down on her lips, and all she could do was struggle to breathe.

"I don't want to hurt you, Ms. Montgomery but if you don't calm down I'll be forced to knock you out." His voice was so flat it sounded almost mechanical and all the more frightening to her ears. "You have a choice. Option A: you make the smallest sound when I remove my hand, my partner over here will give you an injection; it will be just enough to put you out for a few hours. I will then carry you out wrapped in a blanket. Option B: you can get up and put your clothes on. Nod once for option A and twice for B."

Dakota's heart felt like it would burst in her chest as it pumped with fear. She risked a glance over her shoulder and her heart stopped.

"Don't worry, he's alive. Representative Holland just won't be waking up anytime soon."

What Dakota really wanted was Option C. The one where she woke up and discovered this was a nightmare. But the fear of the unknown far outweighed her thoughts of bravery. She could tell by their behavior that the men were professionals and would have no compunction to rendering her unconscious in the same way they did Blake. Hoping that she would be able to glean more information as to why she was their target, Dakota nodded twice. When he took his time removing his hand from her mouth she glared at him as he moved from the bed. And as her wits returned, she committed his likeness to memory. "Who are you and what do you want from me?" Her voice was raspy with fear.

"Call me, Carter. My partner over there is called Mills. We're here to keep you safe, ma'am. Senator O'Connor is about to make some Japanese criminals very unhappy, and he wants to make sure you don't suffer from the backlash."

As she listened to the man's voice, she detected a hint of a Southern accent. Had they met under different circumstances, she would have thought him a gentleman. Aware her thoughts had shifted Dakota readjusted her grip on the comforter. "What is Peter going to do? Nobu has to know that I haven't met with him and couldn't have passed along any secrets."

"I'll tell you all the details once we're on the road, but we need to leave before the next security shift starts. Leave your clothes."

"What about Blake? I can't just leave him."

"Write a note and make it quick."

"What am I supposed to say? Don't worry about me. My adopted brother just had me kidnapped?" she replied sarcastically. Now that her fear for their lives had faded, anger began to work its way into her thoughts. What in the hell had possessed Peter to do something like this? He was the most law abiding person she'd ever known. The most trouble he'd had was speeding tickets, even then as a U.S. senator he was exempt from paying even the most minimal of fines. But to find out he was the person behind her kidnapping? Dakota shook her head. Everything she'd ever thought about her first love changed.

"Make something up. You women are always good at lying."

She aimed a hateful glance at the man's back. Thankful for the small modicum of privacy, she hurriedly dressed and pulled on her shoes. What to say to the man she loved? God, she could imagine what he'd think when he woke up and found her missing. She couldn't tell him about Peter and she couldn't leave him. Dakota walked over to the small table and picked up a hotel pen. What if anything did she write? No matter what note she left, Blake would see her absence as an act of betrayal. She shook her head regardless of how deeply their relationship had grown; there could never have been a happy ending. They were both set in their ways. Blake would want a political wife and she would never be able to suppress her intrinsic dislike of politics. No matter. She sat down and held the pen in her hand but was unable to write.

"Look, Ms. Montgomery, we don't have a lot of time here. You're a journalist right? Just make it look like you needed to leave on an emergency assignment."

She began to write and a moment later jumped when a hand came down on her shoulder. "No time for an autobiography. It's time for us to leave. We've got a boat to catch."

All of a sudden, everything felt wrong. Her head and her heart were in agreement. She shouldn't go. She took a step back and shook her head. "No, I can't leave."

"You have gotta be kidding me," the mercenary groaned.

She shook her head. "No, I'm not going anywhere with you. Tell Peter he'll just have to leave me out of this. Why would Peter think that Nobu would hurt me? Why now?"

He took her arm and began to lead her toward the door. When Dakota attempted to jerk her arm away from his grasp, he cursed. "Look lady, this isn't personal."

Unnerved by the sudden look of pity in the man's eyes, Dakota swung around but was not fast enough. Before she could move, a strong arm clamped around her and something nauseous was placed over her mouth and nose. The world became a blur and everything faded to gray.

Chapter 19

B lake woke with a dry mouth, headache and upset stomach. Barely five minutes passed from sleep to being awake that nausea sent him stumbling through the door in search of a bathroom to hang his head over the toilet as dry heaves racked his body. After he rinsed his mouth, he returned to the room and noticed the silence of the suite. That was when he eyes fell on the note casually waiting on the table.

He picked it up and read it. *Forgive me. I got a call from the bureau. I had to leave for a confidential assignment. I promise to contact you when I can. Dakota.*

A knot twisted in his stomach. His chest contracted and teeth ground against teeth with fruitless frustration. He rubbed his brow as his head began to ache. He hadn't felt this bad since his graduate school graduation party. Blake frowned; he hadn't had anything stronger than a glass of plum wine the night before.

He reread the note, then curled it up in his fingers. She must have found out about Peter. Cursing, Blake got dressed, threw on his jacket, and pulled open the door. It took him only a few minutes walk toward the main resort before he saw a lone man walking in his direction.

"Agent Richards," Blake shouted. "Where the hell is Dakota, and why did you let her leave?"

The man's brow wrinkled. "Sir? As far as I know, Ms. Montgomery hasn't left the suite."

"She's not there," he shouted. "She left a note about an assignment. I want her found and brought back now."

"Yes, sir."

Blake flexed his fingers and waited as Richards placed a phone call. The knot in his stomach tightened with helpless frustration. He was a light sleeper and had been all of his life. How and the hell could he have missed her packing? The more he thought about it, the more he was convinced that something didn't feel right.

"Sir, if you'll wait in the suite, I'll wake the agent on duty, and we'll question the hotel staff," he said in a calm professional manner.

"You do that." He would use other means to find her. Blake recalled the tracking device he'd implanted in her purse. He quickly jogged back to the suite, entered into the bedroom suite, and slid back the closet doors. Immediately he noticed that her luggage had disappeared along with her clothes. Anger crowded his mind, and he went into the other room to boot his laptop.

Dakota Montgomery was a fighter not a coward. If she'd found out he'd kept something from her, she'd have confronted him. Unless she'd somehow discovered that he'd known all about her visit to see Nobu Toshinori. No sooner had the welcome screen come on when someone knocked on the door.

"Come in!" he barked. Blake was ready to explode. While pulling up the website to enter the tracing device identification code, his eyes didn't leave the screen as the hourglass turned.

"Sir, we can't find Ms. Montgomery on the property."

"Don't waste your time," he said shortly. "Her clothes and her luggage are gone."

"True, there's something else."

Blake forced his attention from the computer screen, shaking his head. "What more?"

"We reviewed some security discs from last night. Ms. Montgomery didn't leave willingly. Someone carried her out and placed her in the back on a van."

"Nobu," he said the name like a curse as his anger boiled to the surface. "If he so much as lays a finger on her, he's a dead man."

Just then the computer beeped and his heart jumped with hope. All too soon his hope crashed as his eyes moved from the computer screen to the floor. Dakota's purse sat next to the bed.

Dakota slowly came to her senses. She tried focusing her eyes on the figures standing over her. The first face she looked into after gaining consciousness was Peter's. The second was that of a man she didn't recognize. Her eyes closed again. Her mouth felt like dry cotton, and her head pounded. As the fog that lay over her mind began to clear, she remembered the fear of something being placed over her face. The sharp scent of alcohol before everything went dark. It took her another moment to realize that she'd been drugged.

"Dakota, can you hear me?" Peter asked softly.

She stared at the face that she'd known for years, and it was as if a stranger looked back at her. The shadows under his eyes had aged Peter seemingly overnight. Her tongue darted out over her lips. "Yes."

Between one blink and the next, like magic a bottle of water appeared in his hand. He placed it to her lips, and she drank greedily.

"Slow down. The doctor said a side effect of the chloroform may be nausea," he warned, then moved the bottle away.

She let her head fall back and closed her eyes to ease some of the pain in her head.

"What happened?"

"You decided not to leave with the men I sent to get you out of harm's way."

"And so you had me kidnapped?"

He frowned. "You left me with no other option."

"Blake…"

"He'll wake up tomorrow and see the note you left."

"Why?" she asked flustered. The desire to return to Blake brought her close to sheer panic, but she couldn't move.

"I can't take the chance that Nobu would hold you hostage to use against me."

She managed to shake her head. "I was protected."

"No, you were watched. There's a difference. They wanted to see if I asked you to steal the trade strategy from Representative Holland. I can't take the thought of losing you, little bit. Until this conference is over, I need you to be safe."

It was then that Dakota noticed the slight rocking sensation. Her head turned and looked out the small window at a very busy dock.

"Don't do this, Peter."

"I'm sorry, but I promise they'll take good care of you. Nobu was linked to kidnapping, extortion, blackmail and murder. Even if the Japanese authorities could link him to this, it would be years before it goes to court. I can't take any chances; you'll travel by boat to South Korea tonight. I've got a private plane ready to take you back to Washington. In a week this will all be over and you can see Holland."

Her heart broke as she recognized the look of determination on Peter's face. Blake would never forgive her of leaving. To him her absence would be a betrayal. Marshalling every ounce of energy she could muster, Dakota struggled to sit up. "I'm...not...leaving. Blake needs me."

"This is about more than you and me, Dakota. Nobu will stop at nothing to derail this conference. If he'll use my own son against me, what's to stop him from using you against Blake?"

Her brow wrinkled. "You have a son?"

"He's thirteen. I didn't even know I had one until two weeks ago. Nobu threatened both my son and his mother. When the men I hired managed to track them down and get them out of the country, he promised to kill you unless I delivered the trade strategy."

Dakota flashed back to the morning she met Nobu in his office. All the pieces came together with blinding clarify. "I need to tell Blake."

"He knows."

"How?"

"The Diplomatic Security Agency and the U.S. Trade Office have been aware of everything. I know they wanted me to use you for the trade strategy. I'm sure they never would have let the genuine information fall into my hands. They had everything planned, and they even bugged your purse."

"No," she shook her head. "I know they monitored my phone calls, but that was all."

"My men detected the tracking device when they were following you," he replied.

Her heart sank at the thought. That meant Blake had known about her going to meet Nobu. "I have to go to him, please, Peter," she begged.

Peter bent down and placed a kiss on her brow. "I'm sorry, but I would rather you hate me, than see you killed."

Dakota caught a movement from the corner of her eyes. The stranger moved closer and she saw a syringe in his hands.

"Keep her safe, Brant," Peter ordered.

A tear slipped from Dakota's eyes, and the prick of the needle was the last she knew before darkness took everything away for the second time.

Blake continued pacing the confines of the bullet train even as he felt it slow in anticipation for stopping in the city of Nagoya. After waking up to find Dakota gone from the hotel room, he'd had the agent research every possible manner of transportation to return to Tokyo. In the end, it was the bullet train. After several minutes the train pulled away from the station and reached a steady speed. Even as the countryside passed in a blur out the windows, all he could see was the empty seat in front of him. The sight mocked him. What kind of man was he who couldn't protect his woman? Why the hell hadn't he woken up? Even the knowledge that he'd been drugged did nothing to assuage the riot of anger and guilt. He needed information from the diplomatic security, information he couldn't access from his laptop, but had to obtain.

For all his supposed power as a trade representative, he felt powerless. Frustration gripped his entire body. He never should have agreed to use Dakota as bait. In his superiors' minds, Dakota was nothing more than a sacrificial lamb for the cause of national security, as well as his own political agenda. After all those years of working hard to build a case against the Japanese governments trade practices, they hadn't stopped to think of the possible pitfalls in their plan. While they'd been counting on Senator O'Connor pumping her for information, no one had fully considered Nobu Toshinori a physical threat to Dakota. Dropping into the empty seat, he closed his eyes. Nothing would stop him from getting her back. Nothing. And if it came to the point he would have to choose between protecting U.S. interests and Dakota...

Blake shook his head. He refused to let that happen. Reaching into his pocket, he pulled out his mobile phone and was on the verge of hitting the send key when it rang. "It's about time you called. Did you get my message?" he barked.

"I listened to all three after my assistant pulled me from a Senate hearing," Michaels said.

Blake looked down at this watch. "My train will arrive at Tokyo station in one hour. I want to question him personally."

"Calm down, Blake. We're going to find her."

"You'd better find her before I get to Tokyo, Michaels, or I will tear the city apart."

"I've got people working with the Japanese authorities to arrange a meeting. It's going to take time."

He felt like hitting something, kicking something. Just doing something to get Dakota back. "Damn it, Michaels. We're running out of time. The closer it gets to the trade conference, leverage decreases and his incentive to make Dakota disappear permanently increases. We need to get to him now. I don't care how many diplomatic protocols we have to break, I want Nobu Toshinori brought in for questioning," Blake practically yelled into his mobile phone.

"You know as well as I do we can't bring him in for questioning without proof, and that's something we don't have. Besides, there's nothing to indicate that Nobu kidnapped Ms. Montgomery."

He stopped and his fingers tightened to a death like grip on the phone. He breathed deeply, and when he spoke, his voice was ice cold. "Are you saying that Dakota left on her own?"

"No, damn it. I'm not saying that. I'm behind you one hundred percent, but my hands are tied. I've got every diplomatic security agent digging for information, and I've called in a favor from a buddy at the C.I.A.. Believe me when I say we are doing everything that we can to locate her. But in the meantime, I just got word the Japanese are making noises to members of the World Trade Organization's Ministerial Conference. There's a real risk that even if we get the concessions we want during the conference, they might appeal to the WTO."

Blake's jaw clenched and unclenched. "We'll need to review the domestic support policies and make sure we're in compliance."

"That's correct. And there's a lot more analysis that needs to happen before the conference. Look, Blake, I understand what you're going through. I need you to let diplomatic security handle the situation. If you can't get your head in the game, then Nobu wins."

"Thanks for the pep talk, Michaels." His superior couldn't have missed the heavy amount of sarcasm in his tone.

After ending the call and tossing the phone onto the empty seat, Blake glanced at this watch. Fifty-five minutes until he made it to Tokyo. The waiting would drive him insane because all he could do was remember. Remembered how she'd kissed him, moving her sweet tongue in this mouth, how she'd fought with him, how she'd listened. Remembered how she'd said she loved him.

For a moment his face softened. He almost couldn't believe she'd said the words. Hell, he couldn't believe he'd said them aloud. There was nothing else he could have said because Dakota owned his heart. Before he'd met Dakota, everything was black and white. He hadn't cared about why Peter O'Connor would have wanted to engage in espionage. All he'd wanted was justice. Now he sat there faced with the real possibility that Nobu could kill the woman he loved unless he betrayed his country.

So lost in his thoughts, Blake jerked when he heard his cell phone ring. Reaching over, he quickly picked it up. "Yes?"

"Blake, it's Peter O'Connor."

Although he should have anticipated the phone call, every muscle in his body tensed as he thought the worst. "What do you want, Senator?" he asked, deliberately curt. He couldn't lay the blame for Dakota's disappearance directly on O'Connor's shoulders, but he could be pissed.

"Call off your search, Holland."

Blake frowned. "Call off my search?"

"Yes. Call off your people."

"Where's Dakota?"

"I have her."

Those three words propelled Blake to his feet. Fury consumed him, burned into him and his mind snapped when he remembered the fear, the pain, and the anguish of discovering Dakota missing that morning. "You son-of-a-bitch!"

"Look, I don't have time to argue. Just pull your men back. I'm handling Nobu, and the last thing I need is diplomatic security interfering with a congressional matter."

"Congressional matter, my ass," he bit out. "Where's Dakota?"

"Safe."

Blake inhaled sharply. "I swear to God, I will hunt you down and personally ruin you, O'Connor, if you've hurt her."

"I would rather cut off my own arm than hurt Dakota, Blake. I promise you she's safe from Nobu, and she'll remain hidden until all this blows over."

"I want to talk to her," he said. "Now." One half of him would have gladly wrapped his fingers around O'Connor's neck and squeezed the life out of the man. The other half couldn't get past the sense of relief.

"Is your need to talk to her more important than keeping her safe?"

"No," he replied slowly. Nothing was more important to him than Dakota's safety. Even if he never saw her again, at least would know that she was alive.

"Good. I'll speak with you at the conference."

The line went dead, and Blake pulled the phone from his ear and stared at it. He would deal with the senator soon enough. But now, he needed to set his thoughts of vengeance aside to concentrate on the trade conference. The sooner it ended, the better. Blake Holland was going to get his woman.

Chapter 20

I 've got to hand it to you, Blake. I didn't think you'd be able to pull this off."

Blake turned toward the Chief of the U.S. Office of Trade Representatives, Ben Michaels, and was barely able to be civil. Even after negotiating a more than fair agreement with the Japanese Ministry to allow an increased amount of raw and finished construction materials and equipment in the country, his victory had been hollow. Dakota should have been by his side.

"Thank you, sir." He nodded and glanced out the small window of the private jet. By his calculations they should be flying above the southern tip of Alaska.

"I also have to thank you for putting aside your animosity for Senator O'Connor. He's always had that tendency to rub people the wrong way, but in this age of politics, you never know when someone could be your opponent one day and your boss the next."

Blake flexed his right hand and the sting of his bruised knuckles brought a grim smile to his face. In public, everything had gone according to plan. Senator O'Connor gave the opening speech and participated in some of the general discussions. In private, Blake had come damn close to beating the hell out of the man.

A cabin steward's approach distracted Blake from his thoughts. "Can I get you gentlemen something to drink?"

"Whiskey neat," he replied.

"Little early in the day to start drinking, isn't it?"

Blake eyed the older man whose hair had begun to turn silver. He should have felt a margin of gratitude. Without Michaels he wouldn't have met Dakota. But the hole that had appeared in his gut the morning she'd gone missing swallowed up all of his emotions except anger.

"Depends on which time zone, you're in," he responded coolly.

"Look Blake. I know about what happened with Dakota Montgomery. O'Connor was wrong, but he saved our collective asses. If Nobu had managed to get his hands on the woman, your effectiveness as the lead of this negotiation would have been non-existent."

Blake eyed the man who had nominated him for his position, manipulated Dakota into helping with the trade mission, and damn near succeeded in humiliating the Japanese trade contingent by going public with evidence of espionage. Yet none of it mattered because everything boiled down to his love for Dakota. Michaels' actions had put the woman he loved in danger. He was thirty-seven years old, and in all those years he could count the people he cared for with his fingers and still not reach double digits. Instead of friendship, there was a cold fury in him when he looked at Michaels. "I need time off."

Michaels nodded and returned his attention to his laptop.

"Your drink, sir."

Blake returned his gaze to the window, wishing he could make the private jet fly faster. Soon, he'd be home and sooner, he'd be with Dakota.

The days after Dakota arrived back in the United States passed slowly. She wasn't allowed to leave the townhouse. Her phone calls were screened and she wasn't allowed visitors. Her only access to the outside world came from the computer, and even that was restricted.

Peter had said he'd spoken with Blake and reassured him of her safety, but that gave her little peace. Dakota saw him in her dreams, felt his fingers on her skin only to wake to the rustle of cotton sheets. Some space in her soul lay empty, and her emotions, which had once traversed the scales from high to low, lay still and quiet.

Dakota twirled around in the leather executive chair and looked about the library. The corners of her mouth quirked into a small smile. Every technological device, decoration and accoutrement lay within the three-story Georgetown townhouse. She had no idea who the owners were and just assumed it belonged to a friend of Peters or a corporate lease. From the third floor, the D.C. skyline was hers for the viewing, but she took no pleasure in watching the flickering lights.

She sighed and dropped the fountain pen on the desk and rubbed her eyes. The journal on her desk sat with pages turned, but she couldn't recall a word of what she'd written. According to the newspaper, the conference had ended last night with favorable concessions for the United States.

Blake will be coming back. Just as quickly, the thought was followed up with the reality that he may not be as happy to see her as she would be to see him. It didn't take a rocket scientist to know Blake placed a high value on trust. No matter how she explained away her actions, it all boiled down to the fact that she'd gone behind his back and seen Nobu. The fact that he'd known only made matters worse.

She stood up from the desk, walked through the hallway and took the stairs up to the second floor. In her bedroom, she closed the door and leaned back, letting the silence of the room wash over her, wishing it would take away the sense of loss she'd carried since leaving Japan.

She hadn't even said good-bye.

Shaking her head, she tried not to think about him or about the why's and how's of Blake's behavior. Was he angry? Did he search for her? Was he happy she was gone? Did he truly mean it when he said he loved her or was it just the sex? Or did he not try to contact her because he thought she was in love with Peter? Or could it have been that he'd confused love with passion? Yet, to believe that he'd never loved her would be to believe Blake to be a liar. Domineering, arrogant, stubborn and exasperating—a lot of adjectives described him, but dishonest wasn't one of them. She wouldn't allow herself to believe they hadn't shared something special.

194

She sniffed as a wave of uncertainty hit her square in the chest. Peter had sworn that he'd told Blake everything, and if that were the case why hadn't he called or returned her voicemails? Her brow wrinkled. She was tired of waiting. She'd learned on her father's knee that Montgomerys didn't watch the world turn, they made it move. It was way past time for her to get her life back, and her life wouldn't be complete without Blake. And if that meant going back to Japan, then so be it. Squaring her shoulders, Dakota walked over to the closet. It was time to pack.

For all Blake knew, Dakota had left Peter's safe house and returned to her apartment in Maryland or left on another assignment. Although he'd make a few inquires as to her whereabouts, no one would talk to him. After he'd arrived home from a week of conference de-briefing in New York City, a thousand thoughts went through his mind as he showered and dressed that late afternoon. Yet none were stronger than the compelling need to see her.

On the drive from his home in Alexandria to the address Peter gave him in Georgetown, he debated calling Dakota but changed his mind. He needed an edge with her. As he merged onto the highway, his mind began to formulate a plan.

Less than an hour later, he cut the engine. He pulled a black velvet box out of his pocket and stared at it for a long time. No matter how much he rationalized it, this was a risk and the more he thought about it, old fears and doubts he'd thought buried began to assail him once more, making the decision that seemed so right a week ago suddenly seem wrong. He shook off the thoughts and shoved open the Jaguar door, Blake Holland didn't take no for an answer and tonight Dakota would be coming home with him.

The first time she heard the chime, she'd thought it was the phone. When it happened again, her hands paused from laying a sweater in the suitcase. Dakota's brow wrinkled as she stood up. Someone was ringing the doorbell. She debated whether or not she would answer it, since she was right in the middle of packing. The doorbell rang again, the finger becoming more impatient. It might be Bert, she thought with a twinge of guilt. He'd threatened several times in the past few days, to fly down to D.C. and drag her back to work. It amazed her that after telling him a portion of the details on the events that took place in Tokyo, he still expected her to write a story about Blake. She sighed and headed downstairs.

Without even looking in the peek hole, she shouted. "Go away. Nobody's home."

She unlocked and swung the door open, ready to blast the person on the other side. When her eyes landed on the man standing on the landing, the frown on her lips melted. "Blake," she gasped. All of her misgivings tripled. She'd lied about taking the train to see Nobu. How could she expect him to trust her, especially given his predisposition against journalism.

"Hello, Dakota."

Several heartbeats passed before he spoke again. "Aren't you going to invite me in?"

More shaken than she cared to admit, Dakota held the door open in silent invitation, and he walked into the foyer. Shutting the door behind him, she studied him from underneath her eyelashes. He looked as if he hadn't slept; the shadows underneath his eyes and the hollowness of his cheeks were new. Uncomfortable with the silence, Dakota brushed past Blake and headed toward the back of the townhouse where the kitchen was located.

"Coffee?" she asked over her shoulder as she passed through the living room.

"Nobu Toshinori was arrested this morning." His announcement stopped Dakota dead in her tracks. She turned and stared at him as if he'd lost his mind. Of all the things she'd dreamed of him saying to her when they met again.

"That's great," she replied tonelessly. A few heartbeats passed before Dakota could speak again. "I should have told you about the meeting."

He nodded. "Yes, you should have."

Dakota twisted her hands together and let out a huge breath as hope sprung in her chest. She could have been kidding herself, but Blake didn't sound angry. She turned and met his dark gaze. She could see nothing in his eyes. "I did what I thought was right."

"To protect O'Connor."

She shook her head, slowly. "In the beginning, all I really cared about was saving Peter. But at the end, I wanted to stay with you, but I wasn't given a choice."

"Just like I'm not giving you a choice now."

He took a step closer and stared down into her eyes while brushing his fingertips against the curve of her cheek. "I won our bet."

Biting her bottom lip, she shook her head. "I don't understand."

"Ambassador Stewart was nominated to be the U.N. Ambassador this morning. We made a wager and I won. Will you honor our bet?"

Taken off guard, she responded, "Of course. I keep my promises."

"Hold out your left hand," he ordered.

She hesitated, but the fierce look in Blake's eyes brooked no argument. Her heart squeezed and the air caught in her throat as he opened the velvet box. He took the band out and looked into her eyes. "I can't promise you I won't make mistakes or hurt you. But I can promise you I will protect you, love you and I will spend the rest of my life with you and do everything within my power to make you happy."

A spasm of emotion racked her body; then her mouth formed the words. "I love you, Blake."

His answer to her statement was to place the ring on her finger. Amazingly, it fit. And before she could say anything else, he pulled her into his arms and held her tight. "This was my grandmother's ring. The one thing my mother would never part with. You're mine, Dakota, and I will never let you go," he whispered in her ear.

"You'll never have to."

He pulled back and looked at her with a hungry, fierce gaze. "I'm taking you home," he stated, speaking the words she never thought she'd hear.

"I'm ready," she said softly, sealing her declaration with a kiss that promised a lifetime.

Group Discussion Questions:

1. Was Dakota every really in love with Peter or was it a crush?

2. Technically, Dakota and Blake never worked *together*, but from an outside perspective, both of their actions were close enough to call into question some serious workplace ethics. The question is, should dating within the workplace be acceptable?

3. In this story, Senator Peter O'Connor had to choose between his loyalty to this country and the lives of the mother of his child and his son. If he hadn't been able to pull off the rescue, what do you think he would have done? Which road would you take if faced with the same dilemma?

4. Has Blake truly gotten over his troubled childhood? How did it shape his perspective and personality?

5. How should Blake have confronted Dakota about her secret visit to see Nobu?